RAVENOUS ROSE

BAD GIRLS OF THE WEST #2

SYLVIA MCDANIEL

VIRTUAL BOOKSELLER

GODSEND

I am no one
Nobody to anyone
I am nowhere
No place or anyplace

I am lost here
Wandering endlessly
I am unclear
Wondering constantly

I am beaten
Destroyed and defeated
I am injured
Disabled and damaged

I am useless
Hopeless and helpless
I am feeble
Weakened and withered

God send your sympathy
God send your security
God send your sanctity
God send your Son to me!

Fight Lord!
Those who fight with me!
Contend Lord!
Those who contend with me!
Judge Lord!
Those who judge me!
Forgive Lord!
Those who forgive me!

I was no one
Nobody to anyone
I was nowhere
No place or anyplace

I was lost there
Wandering endlessly
I was unclear
Wondering constantly

God send your sympathy
God send your security
God send your sanctity
God send your Son to me!

This is usually the part of a first-person narrative where the main character tells the reader who he is. But I don't know who I am. Or where I am.

All I know is that I woke up under a bridge with a splitting headache and some crazy-looking dude trying to steal my boots.

"Hey, you!" I yelled, causing another streak of white pain across my skull. "What are you doing?!"

The crazy-looking dude suddenly stopped trying to untie my boot laces and looked up at me in surprise. "Get out of here!" I pleaded, using my boots to kick at the kneeling figure in front of me. "Leave me alone!"

The crazy-looking dude raised both his hands like he was surrendering, but still gave me an evil grin. "Sorry, Mister," he mumbled. "I thought you was dead."

I felt dead, or almost dead anyways. But I felt I needed to keep my boots regardless.

The crazy-looking dude scurried away from me, kicking up a cloud of dust, broken glass, syringes, and other garbage. Through my blurred vision, I noticed that the crazy-looking dude barely had anything covering his feet. I felt a tinge of sympathy for him, especially now that I was sensing the crisp cool air under the bridge.

The ruckus caught the attention of another bridge dweller, an older woman dressed in multiple layers of rags, who reluctantly approached me from an area where others had gathered around a small fire.

"Who are you people?! What have you done to me?!" I screeched at the blurry figures around me.

In fear, I tried to stand up and flee, but I quickly crumpled back down into the littered debris beneath me. My head throbbed like a snare drum and my tightly stretched skin trembled uncontrollably as the strange woman creeped closer.

"Are you okay, sir?" the woman asked, as she tilted her head toward me with a queer skewered look on her face. "You don't look so good. I brought you some water. I ain't even opened the bottle yet. You wanna drink?"

She kneeled beside me and twisted off the top of the plastic water bottle.

"A drink?" I mumbled.

"Yeah, a drink. You want me to hold it to yer mouth?"

"Yes," I blurted out. "Please, yes. I need water.... I don't feel well."

Before I could say another word, I felt cool liquid flow past my parched palate and engorge my gammy gullet, until I choked as if I were drowning in a pool of some kind of electrified elixir. Excess water and dried blood shot from my mouth and nostrils, spraying across the front of my dingy business suit.

The woman finally pulled the bottle back from my lips and exclaimed, "I guess you was thirsty!"

I continued to choke as I rolled over onto my stomach, but then the woman began slamming her hand against my back as if that torture technique would quickly clear my enflamed esophagus.

"I hope you don't need mouth-to-mouth resucksitation!" I heard her yell above me.

"So do I!" I hollered through the hacking.

Soon my stomach sickness subsided, and I rolled back over onto my back, but then my headache roared back. I reached up and grabbed my skull like I was trying to diffuse a bomb.

"My head!" I cried. "What's wrong with my head? Oh, god it hurts!"

"You gotta pretty big bump there, buddy," the woman diagnosed after a quick visual inspection. Thank god she didn't try to touch it!

I gingerly leaned up against an embankment while the woman watched and winced. When I was situated, she handed me the half-empty water bottle.

"Thank you," I whispered.

"Yer welcome," she answered. "We all need some help ever now n' agin."

I took a small sip of water. Yes, I mean a very small sip.

"Where am I?" I asked. "Please tell me where I am."

"Well, yer under the Second Avenue bridge. Don't you 'member how you got here?"

"No," I sighed. "I don't remember. I'm having trouble remembering anything... I think I seriously hurt my head."

The woman stood back up and leaned over to re-assess my injury as I took another small drink. There wasn't much left to consume.

"Yep," she verified her previous prognosis. "You must-ah hurt yer head somethin' fierce, 'cause folks dressed as nice as you don't usually hang out under this bridge."

I looked down at my soiled suit and finally

loosened my necktie with my free hand. I sure wish I had unknotted that neck noose earlier...

I strained my neck to glance up toward the towering torso beside me.

"Say," I said. "Do you think you could help me to my feet? I – I don't know if I can stand on my own."

"I kin sure try" she politely proffered her palm. "Here, take hole of my hand."

I tossed the now empty bottle into the trash heap and reached up to grasp her cold boney appendage. I pushed with my other arm and slid myself up the embankment wall until I was standing... Standing unsteadily, or perhaps lightheadedly leaning, is a better description.

"I made it!" I triumphantly lied to myself.

"You think you can stand on yer own now?" she asked as soon as I loosened my death grip on her poor hand.

"Yes," I lied again. "I think I can even walk."

Backing away, the worried woman warned, "Well, you be careful and take it easy, ya hear?"

"Yes, yes," I lied a third and fourth time. "I'll be careful. Thank you again for helping me."

"Sure thing... By the way, what's yer name?"

"Heck if I know," I yelped with a lurch that took me lurching across the garbage-covered ground.

She called after me, "Hector?"

I soon found myself stumbling along a pedestrian strewn sidewalk. As with the names of all these milling pedestrians, this millennial city was also completely unfamiliar to me. No one would even take a millisecond to listen to a simple inquiry from me, let alone answer a question. I was pushed from the left side of the sidewalk to the right side of the sidewalk, and from the front side and from the back side. I was spun like a cheap top, wobbling across a coarse cement sidewalk.

The only stationary soul I saw was at a bus station. I stopped at the bus stop to speak with a woman, who at first ignored my approach as if she were looking beyond me for an approaching bus.

"Excuse me, ma'am," I quietly said as I gently touched her coat sleeve to get her attention.

Her scream was ear-shattering and did not help my headache. Nor did the police officer who suddenly jumped to her rescue and slammed a night stick into my skull.

***

This is usually the part of a first-person narrative where the main character tells the reader who he is. But I don't know who I am. Or where I am.

All I know is that I woke up in a jail cell with a splitting headache and some crazy-looking dude trying to steal my boots.

"Hey, leave me alone!" I exclaimed, suddenly realizing that I was stretched out on the lower bunk of a small cell and a man was trying to unfasten my footwear. The brutish bully at my feet grinned at me.

"Well, lookie who's awake... Good morning, er, afternoon, Mister Fancypants."

"Wah-what?" I asked, trying to clear my busted and battered brain.

"I said, good afternoon, Fancypants," he repeated his gibberish as he walked around the bunk to lean down into my face. "Ain't you got no manners?"

Then I heard a dim echo from above, "Yeah, huh-huh, ain't you got no manners, fancy mister pants?"

The brutish bully suddenly arched up away from me and cursed at the mystery inmate in the bunk above me. "Shut up, Dim, before I pull you off that bunk and slam you onto the floor!" he warned the man just before I heard the dull thud of fist against flesh.

"Ow!" squalled the upper bunk man. "I did nuthin' to you and ain't nobody pullin' me offin' this bunk."

The brutish bully ignored the redress from the peanut gallery and leaned down to re-address me. "I said, ain't you got no manners?"

"Manners? Who are you anyway?" I courteously inquired.

He spat back, "Nunya bidness who I is! I wanna know what you did to git in here!"

"I don't know how I got here or who put me in here."

"You was drugged in here by one-ah the pigs!"

"Yeah," echoed from above. "One of the pigs."

"For what?" I asked, even though I knew it was rhetorical.

"That's what I want to know!" the brutish bully demanded.

I watched his adam's apple jump up and down in his swollen throat like a failed yo-yo trick, until I finally reached the end of the line and lost my temper.

Apparently, some forgotten instinct came over me and I put all my weight behind a sudden strike to his sweaty throat.

The brutish bully's face turned red instantly and he grabbed at his injured throat with both hands, while violently falling backward against the cell toilet. The inmate from above got in a painful punch to my jaw, but I quickly grabbed his arm and yanked it so hard I think I pulled it from the socket.

As the jaw-breaker's body slammed onto the cement floor of the cell, I screamed, "I thought no one was going to pull you off that bunk?!"

The next morning, I was led by a bailiff into a non-descript conference room. I took a seat at an empty table and stared forward at a blank television screen, positioned precariously atop a flimsy metal stand. I decided at that moment that I must not be a morning person.

A guy in a cheap business suit eventually sat down beside me and placed his cheap briefcase on the table. He then reached over to shake my hand and I obliged.

"Hey, man, what happened to you?" he greeted.

I snorted and answered, as best I could, "I had a disagreement with some other inmates."

He loudly popped open the combination latches on his briefcase, probably all still preset to the factory 0000 combination. "Sorry, what did you say?"

"I got beat up," I mumbled.

"Well, that's not good."

He then made a show of thumbing through some papers inside the briefcase.

I admitted, "I think my jaw might be broken."

He turned to me and repeated, "Well, that's not good."

"You're telling me..." I added, reaching a hand up to massage my miserable mandible.

"No, seriously," he said. "That's not good, because we're going to be talking to the judge in a minute and you're going to have to speak up so she can hear you."

I waited a moment but kept eye contact. "Exactly who are you?"

He perked up a bit and smiled. "Oh, my bad... I guess I failed to introduce myself. I'm your designated public defender."

I didn't return the smile, but I did roll my eyes.

"And do you have a name?"

He returned to his paper thumbing practice and said into his open briefcase, "That's not important. You just need some kind of, of token representation, because that's how the justice system works."

"I don't either."

He glanced at me briefly for clarification. "You don't what?"

"A name," I answered, looking down at the table. "I don't have a name."

"A name?" he said with an encouraging smile. "Of course, you do! It's right here in your case file. I believe it's John something..."

He grabbed a sheet of paper from the stack and I got excited.

"Yep, right here it says your name is John..."
"John what?"

"Um," he answered, reading from the page. "John Doe."

"John Doe?" I sneered.

He looked back at me and explained, "Well, that's obviously not your real name."

"Yeah, obviously."

"They must have just booked you under the name John Doe because you were unresponsive."

"Oh yeah, I was unresponsive all right."

"Well, since you're not currently unresponsive, please tell me your full name for the case file."

Getting a bit aggravated, I reiterated, "I told you, I don't know."

He sarcastically responded, "You don't know whether you want to give me your full name?"

I slammed the palm of my hand on the table. "No!" I emphasized. "I don't know what my name is!"

"Oh," he said with a perplexed look on his face, completely unphased by my outburst. "Well, that's not good."

"I'm telling you, I don't remember," I tri-peated. "I think I got hit on the head and it jarred my memory or something."

"Wow, like I said before…"

"I know, I know, it's not good," I interrupted.

"Yeah, definitely not good!" he agreed. "You know, the judge is going to want to know who you are."

"Not as much as I do."

"You'd be surprised, she's a stickler for stuff like that," he concluded. "Listen, we haven't got much time and we need to go over the charges."

"Charges?" I questioned, then accepted defeat. "Okay, tell me what I did."

Reading from the sheet, "What you did... Okay, here are the charges from the arresting officer... Aggressive Panhandling and Assault."

"That doesn't sound right," I said.

"And it probably isn't right," he admitted. "Because I know this officer tends to exaggerate when it comes to filing charges."

I felt relief that my belief concerning the false charges was correct.

"Okay, so I plead innocent, right?" I proposed as I sat up straight in my chair.

The public defender guy laughed, and then emphatically stated, "Of course not! Don't be silly. You're going to plead guilty as charged."

"Excuse me?"

"You heard me," he advised. "You're going to plead guilty and I'm going to tell the judge it's your first offense. The judge will then let you walk right out of here."

I slouched back in my seat, looked up at the ceiling, and blurted, "But I'm innocent... At least I think I am."

"That's the problem," he explained. "You can't prove it."

I took my eyes off the stained ceiling tiles just long enough to say, "But the defendant shouldn't have to prove his innocence."

He smirked and answered, "You've been watching too much TV, Mister Doe."

"Whatever," I responded, as I sat back up in the chair and sardonically looked toward the blank television screen on the flimsy TV stand. "I may not remember my name, but I think I know how the justice system is supposed to work."

"Not in this jurisdiction you don't," the PD in the second-rate suit advised, completely missing the irony of the TV in the room. "If you were to plead not guilty, the judge is going to call in the arresting officer to testify. The officer will likely be upset, and he will add on additional charges, which the judge will happily believe."

"Okay, okay," I exclaimed, throwing my arms toward the ceiling. "I'll plead guilty."

"Yes, you'll plead guilty... and apologize."

"I will plead guilty and I will apologize."

"That's good."

When his eyes returned to the paperwork, I added, "You still haven't told me your name..."

I doubt he was going to answer, but it didn't matter because the bailiff pointed a remote toward the television and the screen lit up with an angry-looking middle-aged woman's sneering face.

"All rise," the bailiff announced.

I assumed the bailiff was referring to myself and my court-appointed representation, so we both stood up from our seats accordingly. The court clerk must have been somewhere in the same room with the judge, but was conveniently hidden off camera, unless they record this stuff and transcribe it later...

COURT TRANSCRIPT
CITY vs. JOHN DOE

JUDGE: Let's move on to the next case... The City versus John Doe... John Doe?

PUBLIC DEFENDER: Yes, your honor, we're here.

JUDGE: I can see that... What's this John Doe nonsense?

PUBLIC DEFENDER: Yes, ma'am. The defendant is experiencing memory issues as the result of a head injury.

JUDGE: Is that right?

PUBLIC DEFENDER: Yes, your honor.

JUDGE: I was directing the question to the defendant.

JOHN DOE: [incoherent]

JUDGE: What? I can't hear you. Speak up.

JOHN DOE: I said, yes, your honor.

JUDGE: My god, man, what happened to your face?

JOHN DOE: I got beat up, your honor.

JUDGE: While in custody, I suppose.

JOHN DOE: Yes, your honor, when I was in the cell.

JUDGE: And I suppose your head injury and loss of memory is being blamed on the arresting officer.

JOHN DOE: No, ma'am, I didn't say that.

PUBLIC DEFENDER: If I may interject, your honor. At no time did the defendant suggest to me that he was the victim of police brutality.

JUDGE: Fine... So, the defendant is on the record that he does not hold the city responsible for injuries sustained while he was in custody?

PUBLIC DEFENDER: Correct, your honor.

JUDGE: I want to hear it from him.

JOHN DOE: [incoherent]

JUDGE: Speak up, man.

JOHN DOE: I do not hold the city responsible for any injuries I received while in custody, your honor.

JUDGE: Including the arresting officer?

JOHN DOE: Yes, ma'am, including the arresting officer.

JUDGE: Very well. Now, these charges against you... Aggressive Panhandling and Assault... Can the defendant explain to me how he came to be charged?

JOHN DOE: I plead guilty, your honor.

JUDGE: Did I ask you how you plead?

JOHN DOE: Your honor?

JUDGE: Counselor, did I ask the defendant how he pleads?

PUBLIC DEFENDER: No, your honor.

JUDGE: No, I certainly did not. I simply asked the defendant how he came to be arrested.

JOHN DOE: I apologize, your honor.

JUDGE: Very well then. Please enlighten me on how you came to be arrested.

JOHN DOE: And the answer is, I don't remember.

JUDGE: You don't remember?

JOHN DOE: Correct, ma'am.

JUDGE: But you're ready to plead guilty?

JOHN DOE: Yes, your honor.

JUDGE: Well, that doesn't make any sense... Does that make sense to you, Counselor?

PUBLIC DEFENDER: Well, the defendant has the utmost respect for the arresting officer, so he is willing to accept the charges as witnessed by the officer.

JUDGE: Bull crap. I think I know what's going on here with these memory loss shenanigans.

PUBLIC DEFENDER: Your honor?

JUDGE: Yes, the defendant is homeless and was out panhandling, when he saw a police officer and thought he might get himself arrested. Now he wants to become a ward of the state and obtain free mental health care because of his so-called amnesia.

JOHN DOE: Wait... That's not it at all... I mean, I would appreciate some help, but I'm not trying to become a ward of anyone.

JUDGE: Well, you'll get no help from me. I am prepared to accept your plea and sentence you to the one night you already spent in custody.

JOHN DOE: But your honor...

JUDGE: But nothing. Maybe you should consider cleaning yourself up, finding a job and supporting yourself. This case is adjourned.

***

The buildings on all sides of me seemed to blur together as I wandered the city streets. No matter which way I turned, there were more buildings and more confusion. I felt like a rat trapped in a cage. I sensed there might be some cheese up ahead if I could just make the correct turn.

I eventually turned into the doorway of a shop.

"Can I help you?" asked a curious clerk behind a circumspect counter.

"I seem to be lost," I admitted.

"Well, where are you going?"

"Actually, I don't know."

"Are you looking for a cheese shop?"

"Excuse me?"

"I asked if you were looking for a cheese shop, because you're inside a cheese shop right now."

"Really?"

"Really."

"I'd like to find a place where I could maybe clean myself up a bit and rest for a while."

"Well, I wouldn't recommend you doing that here."

"Agreed."

"But there is a city park a few blocks down where you might be able to rest. Just look for a large fountain and you'll be right there."

My empty stomach then reminded me that I was around food.

"Hey, does this cheese place happen to give samples?" I asked.

"Well," he responded. "I think the concept behind providing free samples is for the customer to then buy some cheese, once they try something to their liking."

"I guess I'll be on my way then," I concluded.

"You have a nice day."

To tell you the truth, I don't know if the cheese shop thing happened or not, because I was still in a state of delirium. I did make it to a park, however, and there was a fountain – a humungous monstrosity of a fountain that sprayed colored water up and around from a multi-faceted cement center flume, which looked like an enchanted water park for sprite water fairies.

My curiosity brought me to the water's edge, and I gazed down into the depths of the ever-changing colored wetness. Soon I realized that hidden lights were creating the sprinkling spectrum. Then I noticed the countless coins of whispered wishes scattered deep beneath the surface, probably two feet beneath the surface of the wavy water. And finally, I noticed the tumultuous reflection of my own face.

"Who are you?" I asked aloud, almost expecting the lively fountain to respond. "I don't recognize you, but you sure are messed up. No wonder the judge told me to clean myself."

I leaned down closer to the surface and scooped up some water to splash on my face. As I felt the cool water splashing against my forehead, I also felt hands on my backside and I heard a youthful voice bellow from behind.

"You need to clean more than your face, you dirty bum!"

Before my entire body hit the water, I also heard another voice delivering a high-pitched, pre-puberty, cackling laugh.

My whole body plunged into the festive depths at the base of the fountain. I twisted around and splashed like a demented dolphin. When I managed to sit upright in the pool, I saw my prodding protagonists running away in the distance.

And a park employee managed to see me from a distance.

"Hey, you!" he yelled at me, as the last of the polluted water drained out of my ear canals. "Get outta that fountain right now! What's wrong with you anyways?!"

I tried to slosh my way out of the pool as fast as possible, but the perturbed man got to the fountain before I could escape.

"I said get outta there!" he yelled again, even though he was now almost right next to me.

"I'm getting there," I impatiently answered. "I'm getting there!"

"And don't you steal none of them coins neither!" he warned. "That money belongs to the park!"

"I'm not trying to steal anything," I protested, while I lifted my first leg over the dampened edge. "I was pushed into the water. Didn't you see those teenage boys running away?"

"Like I said, you better not steal nuthin'," he added for good measure as he began to belligerently walk off.

Once I was completely out of the fountain, I thought to myself, I would never steal the devices driving someone else's desires, even if I can't afford my own.

I sloshed and sploshed, and spattered and splattered, my way over to a park bench, and splashed myself onto the dry wooden slats. I felt like a waterlog swimsuit that had been carelessly slung over a beach motel balcony railing without any realistic hope of drying by the next day.

A young couple soon passed in front of me. The young man held the woman's hand with one hand and held a brown paper bag with the other hand. The woman held a cellphone with her free hand.

"Hey, Swampy," the fellow addressed me. "You hungry? We got some food left."

I looked up at him and answered, "I'd be much obliged, sir, thank you."

But, surprisingly, the man continued to walk past me, eventually tossing the bag into an adjacent garbage can.

He looked back at me and grinned. "Then you can work and dig it out of the trash, lazy bum!"

His woman burst out laughing as she held her phone up to capture my shocked expression. Perhaps you saw the clip on social media.

I waited until the couple was far in the distance before I retrieved the bag from the trash can. The bag contained half a sandwich - a cheese sandwich.

The meager meal provided me the energy and stamina to further explore the strange city where I found myself, even though I hadn't really found myself at all. But I set out to meander this mysterious metropolis none the less. After all, I had nothing better to do.

I soon came upon a bland boring building that proved itself to be a government-run establishment. The words "Public Assistance" on the wall piqued my peculiar interest, so I wandered inside the edifice.

A polite-looking social worker welcomed me into her modest office space. Actually, I barged right in and sat right down in the chair opposite her surplus-looking desk. She dutifully checked her wristwatch.

"It's almost five o'clock," she informed me, as if I had asked her the time.

I asked the obvious question, "Do you have a sister who serves as a judge?"

"Excuse me?"

"Never mind, I'm here for public assistance."

"The office closes at five."

"I understand that, but I am still seeking assistance."

"With what?" she politely postured.

"Well, just look at me," I answered, extending my arms to provide a full view of my helpless condition. "I mean, isn't it obvious that I need help?"

The woman smiled politely and replied, "Sir, lots of people drop by their local thrift shop, buy some rags, dirty themselves up, and try to scam the government."

"Well, that's not me," I argued. "I am legitimately in need of assistance."

"You'll have to be more specific, sir."

"I'm homeless, for one," I specified. "And I'm also hungry."

I was provided with another smile and the kind retort, "I didn't hear anything about wanting a job."

I did the obligatory eye roll thing and informed her, "Don't get me wrong, I'm not afraid to work..."

She began typing and focusing on the desktop computer screen, which seemed encouraging to me.

"Okay, then," she began. "Let's begin with your name."

"I don... I don't know."

I swear that I saw her grin as she typed something and responded, "First name, Ida? Spelled I-D-A?"

I sat silently, stewing in a soup chock full of salty righteous indignation, until she finally took her eyes off the computer and reluctantly looked my way.

"I'm not interested in playing word games," I told her crossly. "I am not sure what my name is."

She stared back and answered, "So you want to obtain public assistance without identifying yourself?"

"Please understand that I'm not trying to deceive anyone," I explained as calmly as I could. "I really cannot remember my name or anything else from my past. I was recently injured, or attacked, and I woke up under a bridge with amnesia."

"So, you've been wandering around town with a serious head injury?"

"Yes!" I exclaimed. "And I'm hoping somebody will help me!"

She deliberately blinked her eyes at me once, twice, three times; and then charmingly checked her watch. I watched as she stood up, gathered her coat from the back of her chair, and began walking away from the desk.

The woman casually walked behind me, turned off the light switch for the office, and exited through the doorway.

Still sitting in my chair, within the now darkened office, I cried after her, "Aren't you going to help me?!"

She poked her smiling face around the corner and told me, "I'm afraid it's five o'clock. Thank you for stopping by."

Like a stubborn shadow, I continued to dwell in the darkness.

She then poked a frowning face around the corner. "The office is closed for the day. You'll have to leave now, Mister Whomever-You-Are."

That is when I jumped up from my seat and angrily confronted her. "No! I won't leave here until I get some help! I need help! Why can't you see that?!"

Taken aback by my outburst, she re-entered the room, turned the light back on, returned to her desk and whispered, "Sure, I know you could use some help, but the assistance you need immediately appears to be medical. The nearest emergency room is five blocks away. I pass it on my way home, so if you want me to drive you there, I would be happy to assist."

The off-the-clock social worker not only drove me to the Emergency Room, but she accompanied me inside and told the nurse about my head injury and my inability to pay. To my surprise, the nurse told me that a doctor would see me soon.

"Take care of yourself," the social worker said upon leaving me in the waiting room. She also gave me what appeared to be a sincere smile. The first one I can remember seeing from anyone.

After brutally pressing down on my head wound (I assume to gauge my response), the doctor grabbed my chin and began moving my jaw in jarring gyrations. "You say your jaw hurts too?"

"Mmm-hmm," I replied in anguish.

Once he released my jaw, he instructed, "Open your mouth as wide as you can."

"Ahhhhh…"

" 'Ahhhhh' isn't necessary."

"Sorry, doc."

"Any loose teeth?"

"I don't think so."

The doc, as I liked to call him, had been standing in front of me, flinging around a variety of shiny metal instruments and providing me with an amusing assortment of inquisitive expressions. He finally sat down, and we were seated almost at the same level, me on the examination table and he on a rolling stool.

He put a gloved hand up to his own chin and pre-diagnosed, "Yes, sir, that's one nasty bump you've got there. Are you feeling any dizziness?"

"The dizziness comes in spells," I answered. "When I start to feel dizzy, I usually have to sit down for a while."

"Any blurred vision?"

"Yes, but I don't even remember if I wore glasses. So maybe the blurriness is not from the injury."

"How about indigestion, sick to the stomach?"

"Well, to be honest, doc, I haven't had much to eat to cause any indigestion."

"But you have an appetite?"

"Oh, yeah, you know it!"

The doctor then leaned back slightly, but not enough to fall from the stool. After a dramatic pause, he concluded, "Okay, Mister Doe, you've obviously experienced a concussion. I am going to order a CT Scan for you to determine the extent of any damage to your skull and brain."

I feigned disappointment in my response: "I suppose I'll have to spend the night in this dreary old hospital then."

"Certainly not!" the quack responded. "At least I don't think so... I mean, not unless we find excessive pressure or bleeding on the brain."

"Oh."

"After your scan, you can return to the waiting room," he concluded. "I will come out and tell you the results as soon as I review the x-rays."

It didn't take me long to fall into a deep sleep once I reached the waiting room, and I have no idea how long I slept there. Eventually, I was startled awake by a jab to my side.

"Hey, are you awake, Mister Doe?" asked the doctor as he sat in a seat beside mine.

"Wha-what?" I stirred.

"Oh, thank goodness," the doc reacted. "I thought you were dead."

"Dead?"

"Well, Mister Doe, I have looked at the results of the CT scan and determined that you did indeed experience a concussion and your skull has a slight fracture, which should heal on its own. There is no apparent brain damage. I wouldn't even recommend any stitches for the small cut."

"But what about the amnesia?" I remembered to ask.

"Oh, yes, the amnesia... Well, I'm no brain surgeon or psychiatrist, but what you likely have is called post-traumatic amnesia. I believe you'll eventually begin to regain your memory, but it may take weeks, or even months, to fully recover."

I immediately sat up from my post-nap position to make sure I fully comprehended the doctor's position on my condition. "Weeks or even months to remember who I am?" I asked while shaking my head in dismay.

"Possibly," he reiterated, as he reached inside his white coat to retrieve a small pill bottle. "In the meantime, I have some ibuprofen here to help with the pain. I also suggest you have social services help you find a homeless shelter. You'll recover faster if you're out of the elements."

"This is... This whole ordeal is just so depressing... You can't imagine, doc," I explained while accepting the plastic bottle.

"Well, I do have some good news," he added. "Your jaw looks okay."

Once I had worn out my welcome in the cozy, dry hospital waiting room, I ventured out into the dark loneliness of the unfamiliar city streets. I tried humoring myself that amnesia caused every day to be like a new adventure, seeing all new things and meeting all new people. But I guess I'm not the type to laugh at my own jokes.

After a few blocks of underwhelming adventure, I reached the parking lot of a pizza place. There was a flurry of activity as employees left the restaurant and walked toward their vehicles, calling out various insincere "good night" and "take it easy" salutations.

The last employee to leave the establishment turned off the neon OPEN sign and lugged a large plastic garbage bag out the front door. The waitress managed to carry the heavy bag across the parking lot, place it on the ground, and open the lid of a dumpster long enough to toss the trash inside. The lid slammed down on its own and the woman walked to her car and left the scene with no one remaining to salutate.

But I began to salivate.

Having now mastered the art of retrieving food from trash receptacles, I did not hesitate to limp over to the dumpster and throw open the metal lid.

Climbing inside was a challenge, but I soon found myself tumbling into the tantalizing trash.

Thanks to an overhead streetlight, I was able to locate boxes and boxes and boxes of partially consumed pizza pies. I even entertained the thought of searching for the most appetizing toppings, but realized I was too hungry to care.

I stood up inside the dumpster and began chomping down on a large slice with pineapple, which I thought was a weird topping for a pizza.

When I reached down for another piping-cold slice, I heard a voice yell, "Hey!"

I stood back up, holding a slice with anchovies, only to encounter an odd couple dressed in colorful rags. The tall man had an unlit butt of a stogie protruding from his rotten teeth and the short woman used a cane to remain vertical. She sported decades old tangled hair that looked like a wasp nest.

"Hey!" the man repeated, hobbling closer to the dumpster. "What do you think you're doin' in there?!"

"I'm eating pizza," I admitted, taking another bite.

The vagrant woman stuttered, "You're eatin' our p-pizza, you mean!"

"I think there's plenty here," I offered. "We can share. You want a piece with extra cheese?"

The vagrant man shouted, "No, we ain't sharin' our pizza! This is our dumpster! Ever'body 'round here knows that!"

"Well, I didn't know!" I shouted back. "I'm new to town!"

"That's no excuse!" spat the she-devil.

"Fine," I surrendered. "I'll leave the dumpster right now and won't ever come back."

But as I was conversing with the crone, the man snuck behind the dumpster and threw shut the lid. It came crashing down on my skull and I began losing consciousness.

Before I blacked out, I could hear the man instruct the woman, "Give me your cane, I'm gonna lock him in there."

"Yeah, teach him a lesson," she screeched. "But you owe me a cane if'n you lodge mine into that latch."

Lucid dreams can be frighteningly real and sometimes are not dreams at all. I vaguely remember my dumpster dream. It involved the loud noise that an industrial garbage truck typically makes when it approaches a commercial dumpster and is followed by the strident sound of its hydraulic arms crashing onto the ground. Then there is a sudden jolt when the hydraulic appendages slam into the side slots of the dumpster. A feeling of weightlessness followed, as I felt like an astronaut spinning inside a smelly space capsule. Finally, I crashed to earth.

***

This is usually the part of a first-person narrative where the main character tells the reader who he is. But I don't know who I am. Or where I am.

All I know is that I woke up in a dumpster with a splitting headache and some crazy-looking dude trying to steal my boots.

As it turned out, he wasn't trying to steal my boots, per se, he was just furiously pulling on them and trying to lift me out of the dumpster.

"What are you doin' in there?!" the crazy-looking dude with a fluorescent vest screamed. "Who locked you inside there?!"

"Help me," I managed to murmur, mostly buried beneath a mound of garbage.

Realizing that I was not dead, he released his hold on my boots and commanded, "Git outta there! Git yerself outta there right now!"

I tried to stand upright from the seeping swamp of slop, from which I had sunk, but ended up falling forward into the front of the dumpster and coming face-to-face with the salty sanitation engineer. He grabbed me by the shoulders and somehow managed to yank me from the enclosure. Finally, I crashed to earth.

"I tole you to get outta here!" he demanded from above. "Now git!"

I crawled away slowly, like a snail leaving a trail of stinky slime.

I now felt like a swamp creature, grimacing with insurmountable pain, and effectively terrorizing everyone who crossed my path on the sidewalk during their morning commute. When I saw a drinking fountain at the foot of an ominous overpass, beaming with teeming pedestrians and pooling car traffic, I got the sense that I possessed pain relievers.

I quickly poked into my coat pockets, my pants pockets and my shirt pocket, but came up empty. I desperately patted down my clothing, hoping to feel the shape of a stray pill bottle that could bring me some relief once I reached the drinking fountain.

I saw a garbage truck rumble past me, driving toward the bridge, and I wondered whether it carried any pill bottles inside its steel belly. The sight of the truck caused me to seethe in anger. The sight of everything around me caused me to seethe.

I marched onto the enormous expanse of the bridge, literally knocking other pedestrians out of my way. When I reached the center of the bridge, I suddenly felt a sense of calm come over me. I stopped and looked over the railing. I was standing high above a rustling river – a river that would swallow me up the second I touched its swirling surface.

I looked to my left and right, noticing that no one was anywhere near me, if I were to ascend the railing. I began talking to myself, realizing immediately that it was like talking to a stranger.

"I've got to end this now... I don't know what or who I was before, but I know very well what I've just gone through... I am in constant pain and misery with no one willing to help me. There's only one way that I can finally end this pain... Forget whatever may have happened in the past... I don't even care anymore."

I lifted one leg over the railing and looked down past my wavering boot at the watery depths beneath me. My pain was already beginning to subside, I told myself, a sure sign that I must be making the right decision.

I began to lift my other boot from the surface of the bridge, but it got snagged on something. I tried again, but still could not lift my remaining leg from the bridge side of the railing. In fact, something seemed to be yanking my pant leg.

I took my eyes off the river and looked toward the walkway of the bridge. I heard growling, then focused on the spectacle of a big dog fiercely pulling at my pants with its huge canines.

I kicked at the mongrel, trying to shake it off my leg.

"Hey! Let go! Get out of here! What are you doing, mutt?"

But the determined dog refused to let go and I was forced to painfully twist my body back over the railing and tumble onto the hard cement. The dog then released my pant leg, crawled on top of me, and began licking my face.

"What's wrong with you, boy?" I asked through the slobbers. "Do I have to go find a different bridge?"

I used the railing to pull myself to my feet. I stepped over the dog and began walking in my original direction, still thinking about another bridge and another opportunity to end my misery. The dog must have smelled garbage on my clothes, I concluded.

But as I walked off, I heard the dog barking behind me. I turned around to face the hound.

"What do you want?" I rhetorically asked the barking beast.

The dog motioned with its front paw and its nose, as though it were pointing in the opposite direction, then turned back toward me and continued yelping.

I stretched my arms out in exasperation. "Seriously, you want me to go that direction?"

Ja-wohl, the German shepherd replied in its own special language.

As soon as I began walking back toward the dog, it started leading the way like a true shepherd. "Slow down," I called from behind. "I'm injured, you know… Remember how you dragged me onto the sidewalk? Really, you need to slow down a bit…"

We walked a couple of blocks until the dog stopped in front of a white brick building. A sign above the door read UNION MISSION, and there was a lighted cross on the roof with the words JESUS SAVES displayed within the frame.

"The City Mission, eh?" I asked the dog as it sat in front of the glass door.

He barked in response.

I looked at the door and noticed a "No Pets" paper sign taped to the glass.

"Well, if you want me to go in there, you'll have to wait outside."

The dog immediately stretched himself out on the sidewalk, letting me know that I was expected to go into the building by myself. "Okay," I answered, opening the door, and walking inside.

An elderly man wearing a white-collared shirt and blue jeans greeted me as soon as I walked into the Mission. "Welcome, brother," he welcomed, waving me toward him. "You look injured. Please come in and have a seat."

"Thank you, Father," I replied.

We walked into a large room, filled with tables and chairs. Some of the tables were occupied by men playing cards or board games, while other men sat alone reading or just dozing off.

"Of course, of course. Please sit at this table."

We both sat down at the small table. A sense of gratitude overcame me, just from being treated like a person – and called a brother, no less.

"And what has brought you here today, sir?" the pastor asked.

"A dog," I replied.

"Excuse me?"

"A dog brought me here, straight to your door," I explained. "I was about to hurl myself from a bridge and this dog comes from out of nowhere and pulls me off the railing."

"That's astonishing!" he exclaimed. "So, a dog actually saved your life?"

"Yeah, a dog saved me from taking my life," I admitted. "But I really have no life to speak of... Certainly no life worth saving.

"That's nonsense," he admonished. "God didn't give you a life just for you to end it on your own."

"Then why did God allow me to be injured so severely that I can no longer remember my name or who I used to be?" I asked.

He cautiously responded, "Well, I know at this moment you don't want to hear me preaching about God working in mysterious ways..."

"You got that right, Father," I laughed pathetically.

"Fair enough," he agreed. "How about I get you some food?"

Nodding my head, I answered, "Yes, Father, I am so very hungry."

"Wait right here," he said as he stood up. "I'll be right back."

While I waited for the pastor to return, I glanced around the room at the men trying to occupy their time. No one looked toward me or made eye contact, but I believe they'd just become accustomed to minding their own business.

The pastor soon returned with a tray of food and a cup of coffee.

"Hopefully, this will be to your liking," he said as he placed the tray in front of me.

"I'm sure it will be," I responded, looking down at the food. "Thank you."

The pastor walked behind me and placed his hands on my shoulders.

"Before you begin, let's take a moment to thank God for this meal," he said as I silently kept my head down. "Lord God, Heavenly Father, bless us and these Thy gifts which we receive from Thy bountiful goodness, through Jesus Christ, our Lord. Amen."

"Amen," I repeated.

When he removed his hands from my shoulders, he added, "Take your time, brother. I will be nearby, but I now have to look after the needs of others."

"I'm not going anywhere, Father."

"That's very good, because I'd like to talk with you more once you've finished your meal."

The meal placed before me consisted of a bowl of steaming stew and a cold cheese sandwich. I scarfed down the cheese sandwich first because the stew appeared too hot to eat. The stew's meaty aroma kept tempting me, however.

When I decided to consume the stew, I carefully placed a paper napkin on my lap. Some of the stew meat ended up in the napkin when I was certain that no one in the room was watching me. I eventually drank the remaining broth directly from the bowl, folded up the napkin and walked out of the Mission.

Once outside, I was pleased to find the German shepherd still lying on the sidewalk.

"Here, boy," I said as I kneeled closer to his level and unfolded the napkin. "Look what I brought for you."

The dog excitedly wagged its tail and began to eat the meat as soon as it was placed in front of him. As I watched the dog gleefully gobble up the stew meat, my eyes began to tear up. Almost on cue, the pooch looked up at me.

"Thank you, boy," I cried. "Thank you for saving my life. You've given me hope. Thank you, so much."

When the dog finished licking its chops, it pounced on me, almost knocking me over, and began licking me with its beef-enriched saliva slapping me across the lips. I sure could've used a clean napkin.

Upon returning to the large room within the Mission, I saw the pastor seated at the same table where we had previously been. The food tray had been removed, but the half-empty coffee cup remained.

The pastor seemed pleased to see me return to the table.

"Oh, thank God, you've returned," he said with a sincere smile. "I thought you might have left us for good."

"Of course not," I answered while taking a seat. "You said you wanted to continue our conversation."

"Indeed, I do," he confirmed. "In fact, this is the time when I usually ask our new guests what their name is… But I know you can't tell me that."

"Not at this time," I agreed, shaking my head in dismay. "I think it might be awhile before I regain my memory… If I ever do."

"So presently, you have no recollection of events prior to your injury?"

"Correct, Father."

"That raises an interesting theological question that I must ask."

"Okay…"

The pastor leaned across the table and whispered, "Do you know if you've been Saved?"

"You mean Saved by the Lord?" I asked.

"Yes!" he excitedly raised his voice. "Born again!"

I repeated, "I said I had no memory prior to my injury."

"I know, I know," he insisted. "But this is different. If you've been Born Again, Jesus entered your heart and soul… and He should still be there. He should still be there, making his presence known."

I frowned and confessed, "I know what you want me to say, of course, to validate your beliefs, but I'm just not sure."

"I remember the day I asked Christ to enter my heart, but even if I didn't remember, I think I would still know that He was there. He's there, guiding everything I say and everything I do," he affirmed.

"He may be with me also, Father, guiding me," I responded. "But He isn't currently making His presence known."

The pastor contemplated my response and then asked, "Do you pray?"

"Not lately, Father. But I may have prayed in the past."

"Even with your loss of memory, I'd like to think you would have tried prayer during your recent tribulations, especially if you had previously been introduced to Christ."

"I'd like to think I was Born Again, but maybe I haven't. I mean, just look at me. Do I look like someone who has been guided by Christ?"

"Looks can be deceiving, my brother," he cautioned. "For instance, my heart tells me you're a thoughtful, gentle man who cares about others... A head injury doesn't bring about sudden empathy."

"I know that I have no malice toward anyone who has mistreated me," I agreed. "In fact, I feel sorry for folks who can be so cold-hearted and mean-spirited."

"Your words are reminiscent of Christ and spoken like a true Christian," he observed. "That's why I can't help but believe you are Born Again."

"If you say so..."

"As Christ was dying on the cross, He forgave those who tormented Him," he continued. "You have the same attribute of forgiveness within you."

"But are you suggesting that a person cannot be gentle and forgiving unless they have Christ in their heart?"

"Of course not," he insisted. "I know there are agnostics whose nature is to treat others with love and kindness. I just think your compassion is more in line with Christian faith."

"Like I said," I professed. "I'd like to think I've been Born Again.

The pastor reached across the table to grasp my hands and urged, "Look inside yourself, my son. Pray with me..."

I respectfully lowered my head and tried to concentrate on the pastor's words, ignoring the burgeoning pain that attempted to distract me.

"Heavenly Father, if this good man has accepted You into his heart, please make Your presence known to him. For once he is certain he has been Saved, perhaps other fond memories will come back to him and fill his soul with joy. Just as Christ rose again from the crypt to live again, we pray that our friend rises out of his state of amnesia to live the life that he once lived. Amen."

"Amen."

We simultaneously raised our heads and made eye contact. He gently released my hands and offered, "I assume you would like a bed for the night."

"I would be most appreciative," I admitted.

"I'll also take you down to the clothes donation room to see if anything fits you."

"Thank you so much."

"And in the morning," he added. "I hope you'll join us in the chapel for a sermon."

"I certainly will, Father."

***

I awoke early the next morning within the Men's Dormitory and quickly glanced under my assigned cot. To my relief, no one had tried to steal my boots. After a shower, I shaved and put on the clean clothes that the pastor had given me. I felt like a new man when I entered the chapel, despite the dreams I had that night.

The chapel was simply a small room with some folding metal chairs, which faced a chipped-up wooden podium. There were a handful of men and women waiting patiently for the pastor to arrive.

It was not long before the pastor made his entrance and walked confidently to the podium. I felt his hand lightly touch my shoulder as he passed.

"I'm sorry we have no hymnals or musical accompaniment," he announced to the congregation. "But if you know this hymn, I hope you'll sing along with me."

He began singing the words:

Amazing grace, How sweet the sound
That saved a wretch like me.
I once was lost, but now I am found,

Was blind, but now I see.

At first it seemed that only the pastor was willing to sing the song, but then I heard a few others join in during the second verse.

'Twas grace that taught my heart to fear,
And grace my fears relieved.
How precious did that grace appear
The hour I first believed.

The lyrics seemed vaguely familiar to me and I sensed that I knew some of the words which followed.

Through many dangers, toils and snares
I have already come,
'Tis grace has brought me safe thus far
And grace will lead me home.

Yes, I really sang that final line! Perhaps grace will lead me home – or at least lead me through this refrain! I continued singing, as if I had just practiced the song as part of a choir.

The Lord has promised good to me
His word my hope secures;
He will my shield and portion be,
As long as life endures.

The pastor heard my familiar voice and looked over at me as if he knew I would soon be singing along with everyone else in the chapel.

Yea, when this flesh and heart shall fail,
And mortal life shall cease
I shall possess within the veil,
A life of joy and peace.

I stood up and raised my voice to complete the now familiar closing lyrics of Amazing Grace; and I was touched to see the pastor leave the pulpit and walk toward me, singing the words that we both knew so well.

When we've been there ten thousand years!
Bright shining as the sun!
We've no less days to sing God's praise!
Then when we've first begun!

The pastor and I were hugging each other by the final line, tears flowing down both our cheeks. I heard applause all around me, like the congregation knew my struggles. Or was it the sound of angels that I heard?

When the pastor released me, I collapsed onto my seat, overcome by emotion. He slowly returned to the podium, his eyes red and his hands trembling. He took a deep breath, carefully opened a book on the lectern, and began his sermon:

One of the miracles that God gives us every day is the birth of a child. Whether it be the birth of a son or daughter, or a grandchild - or our own birth.

Of course, no one asked us if we wanted to be born,

or to whom we wanted born. From the moment we left the womb, we were suddenly thrust into an environment where we needed to learn to survive.

We may have been born into a poor family, or an abusive family, and wondered why God would place us there, instead of in a grand mansion surrounded by nannies who would feed us the best baby food from silver spoons and fine china.

But the greatest of God's miracles is not our physical birth, but our Spiritual birth. Yes, I say that the Spiritual birth of a lost sinner into spiritual life is the most miraculous gift that God offers mankind!

Why is Spiritual birth more miraculous than physical birth? Because when we are Born Again, God allows us to escape the pains of Death in this life and grants us Eternal Life in Heaven.

When I was a student in seminary, my instructor, Father Jon Daniels, asked the class to describe the essence of being Born Again. We students all knew that we were Born Again and had Christ in our hearts, but we had great difficulty in putting the experience into words.

I still have my notes from that day, and this is how Father Daniels explained the Spiritual state of being Born Again: "To be born again doesn't mean that a good person just becomes a really good person... Or that a moral person just becomes an even more moral person... Or that a church member simply becomes an even better church member. To be Born Again means that a spiritually bankrupt person gains all the promises and blessings that God promises to those who are His. It means that a totally depraved, wicked person is completely cleansed of all his or her sins. It means that a person who has absolutely nothing to offer to God is freely given the greatest gift that they could possibly receive, and that is Eternal Life. It means that someone who is completely and totally rotten to the core becomes a child of God. Who is that spiritually bankrupt person, that totally depraved wicked person, that person who has absolutely nothing to offer to God? That person who is completely and totally rotten to the core? That person is you. That person is me."

Now I would like to read from John, Chapter Three, Verses one through eight: Now there was a Pharisee, a man named Nicodemus, who was a member of the Jewish ruling council. He came to Jesus at night and said, "Rabbi, we know that you are a teacher who has come from God. For no one could perform the signs you are doing if God were not with him."

Jesus replied, "Very truly I tell you, no one can see the kingdom of God unless they are Born Again."

"How can someone be born when they are old?" Nicodemus asked. "Surely they cannot enter a second time into their mother's womb to be born!"

Jesus answered, "Very truly I tell you, no one can enter the kingdom of God unless they are born of water and the Spirit. Flesh gives birth to flesh, but the Spirit gives birth to spirit. You should not be surprised at my saying, 'You must be Born Again.' The wind blows wherever it pleases. You hear its sound, but you cannot tell where it comes from or where it is going. So it is with everyone born of the Spirit."

The pastor then closed his Bible and asked the congregation, "Tell me, brothers and sisters... Is there anyone here this morning who wants to hear the sanctifying sound of God's breath blowing through their soul?"

Everyone, except the pastor and I, silently left the chapel. The pastor took a seat next to me. I began sobbing on cue.

"Last night I had the most horrific nightmares, Father," I cried. "They were so vivid and so real to me... I was a young man in the dreams, and I did terrible things."

"They may have only been dreams, my son, with no basis in reality or your past," he attempted to comfort me. "Everyone has bad dreams every once in awhile."

"But I can't take the chance that I possibly could have done any of the sinful things I saw in my dreams," I confessed. "I feel like, if I had sinned that way as a young man, then Christ would have forgiven me upon my being Saved - and I would no longer be troubled by such nightmares."

"Perhaps your injuries are causing your troubled dreams," he suggested, placing his arm around me.

I lowered my head and prayed aloud, "Dear Lord Jesus, I know that I am a sinner, and I ask for Your forgiveness. I believe You died for my sins and rose from the dead. I turn from my sins and invite You to come into my heart and life. I want to trust and follow You as my Lord and Savior... Amen."

The pastor paused and then asked, "Where did you learn that?"

I lifted my head, turned toward him, and said, "I saw it on a pamphlet last night and memorized it. Did I say it right?"

"You said it fine," he answered, "but as you were reciting what is commonly called 'The Sinner's Prayer,' God enlightened me about something that is very important."

"Please enlighten me," I urged.

"The prayer is fine, even though it is not in the Bible," he explained. "But please realize that inviting Christ into your heart is just the beginning. You must continue to have faith and to act accordingly. A man can only be saved through faith. And faith is much more than repeating a formulaic prayer. Salvation is achieved through acts of faith."

I stood up and declared, "From this point forward, I shall walk in faith with my Savior, Jesus Christ."

But the boldness in my stride and the conviction in my heart began to falter as soon as I stepped out of the Mission door. I panicked as I looked in every direction. Throngs of people and lines of cars blocked my view.

"Boy?!" I yelled.

Yelling above the spin of the pedestrians, "Boy?!"

Yelling above the din of the traffic, "Boy?!"

Yelling above the sin of the world, "Boy?!"

I leaped to the left side of the building, pushing past everything in my path. I raced to the right side of the building, weaving wantonly through everyone in my way. I dropped to my knees on the corner and asked God, "Where is my dog?"

Of course, as soon as I asked, the darned dog nearly knocked me over.

***

Although my time there was not completely callous, we walked together to escape the cruelty of the city. And even though there had been a fracas at the fountain, we walked together to seek peace within the park.

While walking around the perimeter of a tennis court, we found the fortune of a lost tennis ball. Neither of us tired of the toss 'n fetch routine; and if I had a tail, I would've been wagging it too.

One of my throws landed at the feet of a park maintenance worker, who was stabbing at trash with a stick and depositing the pierced pieces into a plastic bag. He leaned down to pet the dog when it arrived to get the ball.

"Sorry, sir," I apologized as I approached. "I hope I didn't hit you."

"Nah, you didn't hit me," the gracious young man greeted. "Nice dog you got here."

"Yeah, he kind of adopted me," I admitted.

"Well, nice meetin' you, but I gotta get back to work," he said. "This trash ain't gonna pick itself up."

"Hey," I inquired, "how do you get a job like yours?"

"You mean picking up garbage all day?"

"Yeah," I observed, "it doesn't look that hard, plus you're out in the fresh air and getting exercise…"

The man laughed and answered, "There's no fresh

air when you're lugging around a heavy bag of smelly garbage and dog poop! Besides, the maintenance supervisor only pays thirty bucks a day."

"Cash?" I asked.

"Yeah, it's all under the table," he admitted. "I think the supervisor lady believes she's helping the less fortunate by letting people like me do her job, while she kicks back in her air-conditioned office."

"Wow," I surmised. "It sounds like you might be thinking about quitting?"

The groundskeeper lowered his burden to the ground and responded, "Actually, I have been... In fact, if you're interested in the job, I'll hand over my rod and my bag, and you can go check in at the supervisor's office near the public restrooms over there."

I was stunned. "Seriously, I can have your job?"

"Hey," he concluded. "At least I found my own replacement, instead of leaving the supervisor high and dry."

"Thank you," I said as I leaned down to pick up the tools of trade. "Your rod and bag comfort me."

"What?"

"Never mind, it was a joke between me and my friend here."

The dog howled in acknowledgement.

I entered the park manager's office, proudly wearing the groundskeeper's fluorescent vest. The middle-aged woman pretended to be busy behind her cluttered desk.

As soon as the manager laid eyes on me, she

discerned, "Don't tell me another one quit?"

I smiled and confirmed, "It appears so, but I'm ready and willing to be his replacement."

"Okay, fella," she greeted as she returned my smile. "Come in and take a seat."

I sat down opposite her and added, "Thank you, ma'am, I appreciate this opportunity."

"You down on your luck, fella?" she observed.

"I guess you could say that," I explained. "One day I woke up under a bridge with a head injury and I haven't been the same since."

"No family or friends to help you?"

"That's the thing," I expounded, breaking eye contact and looking down toward the floor. "The injury caused amnesia and I can't remember who my family is, if I even have one."

"Well, I'll help you out, at least as far as a job."

"How about shelter?" I pressed my luck as I looked back up at the kind woman. "I noticed the attached garage. Can my dog and I sleep there until I regain my memory and get back on my feet?"

She grinned and agreed, "Hmmm, I suppose so, as long as you don't make a mess of the place or take anything."

"Oh, no ma'am," I pledged, "you won't even know that we're sleeping there."

"Okay then, did my ex-employee explain to you what the job entails?"

"I assume it's keeping the park clean from garbage."

"And dog poop," she added.

"And dog poop," I reiterated.

"Also disposing of the trash in the dumpster behind the restrooms. There's a surplus of plastic trash bags in the garage."

I hesitated.

"Wait," I cautioned. "Is there a lock on that dumpster?"

"Why do you ask?" she asked with a confused expression.

"Oh, never mind," I answered. "I guess that was a silly question."

"Yes," she slowly added. "Well, the job pays thirty dollars cash, per day. Is that acceptable?"

"That'll keep me and my dog from going hungry," I accepted.

We both rose and shook hands on the deal.

"Welcome aboard!" she announced. "Oh, fella, did I get your name?"

"I don't have a memory of one yet, but I guess John will do for now."

"As in, John Doe?" she realized.

"Actually, I'd like to think more along the line of John Three-Sixteen."

She walked around the desk and hugged me, whispering, "For God so loved the world that He gave His one and only Son, that whoever believes in Him shall not perish but have eternal life."

"Yes, ma'am," I witnessed.

***

So, there I was the next morning, cheerfully poking at whatever trash I found on the park grounds, when I came across a cellphone amongst the leaves and debris. I looked up and saw a young couple walking away with their backs toward me. I assumed the phone belonged to one of them, so I followed the couple.

As soon as the couple took a seat on a park bench, I recognized them from our earlier encounter.

"Excuse me, folks," I announced upon my approach. "But did one of you just drop your phone?"

The young woman was pleasantly surprised and accepted the phone from me. "Why thank you, sir!"

"No, problem," I said. "I'm glad to be of service."

"Yeah, thanks, dude," the man agreed with a grin. "She's ain't nuthin' without her phone."

"Well," I added, making eye contact with the man, "I also never got to thank you for the food you put in the trash can for me."

The astonished woman elbowed the man in the side and told him, "You apologize to that man right now for what you done!"

The man stammered, "Oh, dude, was that you? I am so sorry for that. Me and my girl were having a bad day and I'm sorry I took it out on you."

"Looks like him and me are gonna have another bad day," the woman grumbled to herself.

"No need for apologies," I explained. "I've forgiven anyone who has ever slighted me."

The trembling man rose from the bench and shook my hand. "I appreciate that, man. In fact, I'd like to buy you a proper lunch today, if you're willin'."

"That won't be necessary, because I've got a job now," I informed him. "But next time you see someone down on their luck, please offer them the meal that you just offered me."

"Will do," he agreed as he sat back down.

"You two have a great day," I concluded as I turned from them.

As I walked away, I heard the man tell the woman, "You laughed too when I threw that food in the trash, so don't act all high and mighty with me."

The woman responded, "I laughed at first, but then I felt bad when I seened the poor man dig in the can for our food. I even prayed God forgive us for mistreatin' that man... I bet our meetin' today shows that both the man and God forgave us."

I believe I then heard him add, "Honey, I think you might be right."

Around midday, I took a break and sat on the edge of the grand fountain. I unscrewed a plastic bottle of water and took a swig. I was going to give the dog the next drink from the bottle, but he must have been thirstier than me because he just jumped over the cement barrier and began lapping up the water inside the fountain.

The fountain reminded me of how the groundskeeper, who had kindly offered this job to me, had failed to recognize me as the man he previously chased out of the fountain. The young couple at the bench also did not recognize me until I introduced myself.

It fascinated me that people often treat others depending on the circumstances surrounding their encounters. In my previous encounters with the groundskeeper and the young couple, I did not appear to be in a favorable disposition, plus I was dressed in drenched and dirty duds.

Of course, some people are just plain mean, regardless of the circumstance...

Two boys rushed me from both sides, the older one shouting, "Let us help you get a big gulp from the fountain, Boomer!"

Their arms were stretched out to push me over the edge of the fountain, but before they could make contact with my shoulders, the dog leaped out of the water behind me and managed to tackle both of the boys at once. Their bodies struck the sidewalk hard and they began screaming in cynophobic fear.

I don't know if the dog actually bit either of them, but it graciously allowed the boys a moment to jump up and run away.

"Stay here, boy!" I yelled to the dog, although I did not believe the dog was going to give chase. "Let them run home to mommy."

But the stubborn duo apparently did not run home to their mother, because I had yet another encounter with the boys before the day was through.

At dusk I carried the last of the full trash bags to the dumpster behind the public restrooms. As I turned to walk toward the maintenance garage where the dog and I had been staying, I noticed that the pedestrian side door was open, and the light was on inside.

"I know I closed that door..." I mumbled to myself.

As I walked closer, I vaguely heard someone inside the garage mention a chainsaw.

When I walked into the narrow doorway, I definitely saw the two teens and I heard the younger one say, "Okay, let's get out of here!"

"Hey," I interceded, "what are you guys doing?!"

"Dammit!" squalled the younger teen.

The older teen was holding the chainsaw and he quickly pulled the cord. The chainsaw buzzed to life and the boy started to approach me, his incoherent cohort cowering close behind him. The noise from the saw inside the garage was almost deafening.

"Git outta our way or I swear I'll cut you in half!" warned the aggressor.

My eyes met the teen's eyes in a defiant stare as I stood my ground. The teen continued to approach me with the screeching chainsaw.

Ignoring my stare, he threatened, "I thought I tole you to git out of the way!"

I courageously walked toward him as he continued his awkward approach. I refused to look down at the spinning teeth of the chainsaw.

"I ain't kiddin' around!" he hissed in anguish. "You better move yerself before you git cut!"

When I felt the blade slice into the front of my shirt, I saw the saw instantly cease its ashen ascent. The saw sputtered and smoked and stalled to a sudden stop.

"What the hell?" the older boy wondered aloud as he looked down at the suspended saw.

From behind the older boy, a small scared voice uttered, "What happened? Why'd you stop?"

"I don't know," the older one admitted. "Maybe the chain came off or it ran out of gas..."

I interrupted, "Or maybe my Lord and Savior Jesus Christ protected me."

"What?!" he questioned.

"You heard me!" I yelled back as I pointed to the rear of the garage. "NOW... PUT...THE... SAW... BACK... ON... THE... WALL."

The younger one pleaded with his partner, "Just do it, brother. Put the saw back."

In acquiescence, he agreed, "All right, all right, I'll put back the saw."

After the teens placed the chainsaw back on the shelf, they both turned to me as I fully entered the garage.

"When I accepted this job," I explained, "the manager said I was responsible for everything inside the garage. If anything came up missing, I'd probably get fired."

"So, you'd rather risk losing your life than losing your job?" asked the older boy.

I countered, "And you'd rather kill someone in order to steal a rusty old chainsaw?"

The younger boy begged, "Listen, Mister, we learned our lesson, so please let us leave."

"Yeah, we learned our lesson," echoed the other.

"Let me ask you this first: How much money do you think you could've got out of that chainsaw?"

"I don't know, maybe twenty bucks," the senior one admitted. "So what?"

"Because I've got twenty dollars right here," I said as I reached into my pants pocket. "If you need it that badly, I'd be glad to give it to you."

"You'd give us twenty dollars?" the younger boy

asked after his jaw dropped open.

"After I just tried to cut you up?" added the other boy.

"If I had more cash, I'd give you more," I told them as I handed over the double saw buck.

The young boy's eyes began to tear up as he admitted, "Our mom could sure use the money, sir."

"Thank you, sir," the other agreed. "We have a little sister that mom needs to feed."

"You know," I observed, "there's plenty of places that would hire able-bodied young men like you."

"That's what our mom keeps sayin'," whichever one said. "But I see now that our way of earnin' cash ain't gonna fly no more."

"Listen, guys, if you meet me at the Mission for the church service at eight a.m. tomorrow, the Pastor can tell you who is hiring around town."

The teen in front turned around to face his brother and nodded to him.

"We can do that."

I stepped aside and allowed the teens to pass. Once they were gone, I prayed, "Dear God, help those boys choose the path of righteousness. Amen."

I then looked around the garage for another missing object.

"Boy," I called. "Where are you, boy?!"

The dog crawled out from under a cabinet.

"Is that where you've been hiding during all the commotion?"

***

Early the next morning, the pastor and I sat at our usual table and chatted before the sermon.

"So, where have you been staying, my son?" he asked.

"God blessed me with a job as a groundskeeper at the city park," I answered. "The manager allows me to sleep in the maintenance garage."

"Well, you're always welcome here, you know that."

"Yes, but if I have a place to stay, I don't want to take up a bed here if someone needs one."

"Of course," he agreed with a nod. "But I do appreciate you dropping by now and again."

"Yes, and I invited two young men to the sermon today," I reported. "They are looking for work and I hope you could give them some leads."

The pastor laughed and exclaimed, "Well, as long as they know their own names and have social security numbers, it'll be a lot easier to place them!"

"That's what I figured!" I laughed along.

When the two teen brothers approached our table, I stood up and greeted, "Well, speak of the devil... or former devils... Here are the young men I was talking about, Pastor."

The pastor also stood and motioned down toward the chairs. "Gentlemen, please take a seat!"

The teens shyly sat down, following our lead.

"I hope we ain't delayin' your service any," one said to the pastor.

"The sermon can wait," he said. "The Lord has more pressing work for me to do."

"Yes," I agreed. "I'm glad you could make it, guys."

"Mom was grateful for the money you gave us," added the other.

"No problem."

The pastor asked, "Are you boys still in school?"

"Not right now, because of summer break. But this fall, I'll be a junior and my brother here will be a senior."

"That's great!" the pastor responded. "So, as far as working hours, I guess you'd be pretty flexible until school starts."

"I don't think it'll matter," one said, lowering his head.

"Why do you say that?" the pastor asked.

"Because we don't think anyone would want people like us workin' for them."

"Yeah, nobody wants us," the other brother agreed. "Not even our father wants anything to do with us."

"Before our dad left us, he said we was all worthless and didn't want to see us no more."

I looked solemnly to the pastor and then to the teens. "I can assure you boys, you're not worthless to God."

"Your friend here is right," the pastor agreed. "You're not worthless. Not to God, and not to either of us. We see your potential and that's why we want to help you."

"Well, we ain't no good in school neither," admitted one boy through tears. "We barely pass each grade. So, who would want to hire a couple of dummies?"

The pastor shook his head and asked, "My son, do you think your brother is dumb?"

"Course not!" he exclaimed.

And then I asked the other, "And do you think he's a dummy?"

"No," he answered. "But other people think we are because we don't do good in school. Even the teachers say they're just pushin' us through to git rid of us."

The pastor instructed, "Don't concern yourself with what other people think."

"Yes," I agreed. "Instead of dwelling over what other people think, you should be spending your time proving them wrong. Your priority right now should be helping your mother. It sounds like she needs you guys even more than you might believe."

"That's why we decided to come here after you helped us out," the older boy cried out as he reached over to grab my hand. "Please forgive me for wanting to hurt you! I am so sorry! I swear, I wish I was dead!"

"My God, boy," I admittedly broke down and covered his hand with my other. "Don't ever say that! I promise you, all is forgiven from last night!"

Recognizing the emotional level at the table, the pastor grabbed the hands of the other trembling boy. "Yes, my sons," he comforted them. "You are both good in the eyes of the Lord!"

After a brief pause, the younger boy asked, "Can we be excused for a moment?"

"Of course," the pastor agreed. "You're welcome to wait for us in the chapel."

The sobbing teens left the table and headed for the sanctuary.

The pastor watched them depart and then turned to me and admitted, "I don't know what happened last night - and maybe I don't want to know."

"Believe me, you don't..."

When I entered the chapel, I saw the teens seated in the front row. I sat down next to them and we waited patiently for the pastor to begin his sermon. Still visibly shaken from our meeting at the table, the pastor took a deep breath at the podium and began:

Even though He had done many good deeds and had helped many people, Jesus was not initially regarded as the Son of God. His fellow Jews ignored His righteous acts and tried to use His words against Him. While attending a celebration inside a temple, other Jews demanded that He declare Himself the Son of God. Jesus answered, "The works that I do in my Father's name bear witness about me, but you do not believe because you are not among my sheep. My sheep hear my voice, and I know them, and they follow me. I give them eternal life, and they will never perish, and no one will snatch them out of my hand. My Father, who has given them to me, is greater than all, and no one is able to snatch them out of the Father's hand. I and the Father are one."

When Jesus left the temple, His detractors followed Him outside. They had taken issue with Jesus's comment that He and the Father are One. They began to collect rocks with the intention to stone Jesus to death. Jesus faced the angry men with the stones and said, "I have shown you many good works from the

Father; for which of them are you going to stone me?" The men answered, "It is not for good work that we are going to stone you; but for blasphemy, because you, being a man, call yourself God."

Jesus responded by asking, "Do you say of him whom the Father consecrated and sent into the world, 'You are blaspheming,' because I said, 'I am the Son of God'? If I am not doing the works of my Father, then do not believe me; but if I do them, even though you do not believe me, believe the works, that you may know and understand that the Father is in me and I am in the Father."

The angry men then looked at one another and realized that no one wanted to cast the first stone, so they dropped their rocks and allowed Jesus to leave unmolested. That story is from John, Chapter Ten.

Jesus had more to say in this Chapter, which I would like to read to you now: "Truly, truly, I say to you, he who does not enter the sheepfold by the door but climbs in by another way, that man is a thief and a robber. But he who enters by the door is the shepherd of the sheep. To him the gatekeeper opens. The sheep hear his voice, and he calls his own sheep by name and leads them out. When he has brought out all his own, he goes before them, and the sheep follow him, for they know his voice. A stranger they will not follow, but they will flee from him, for they do not know the voice of strangers. I am the door of the sheep. All who came before me are thieves and robbers, and the sheep did not listen to them. I am the door. If anyone enters by me, he will be saved and will go in and out and find pasture. The thief comes only to steal and kill and destroy. I came that they may have life and have it abundantly. I am the good shepherd. The good shepherd lays down his life for the sheep. He who is a hired hand and not a shepherd, who does not own the sheep, sees the wolf coming and leaves the sheep and flees, and the wolf snatches them and scatters them. He flees because he is a hired hand and cares nothing for the sheep. I am the good shepherd. I know my own and my own know me, just as the Father knows me and I know the Father; and I lay down my life for the sheep. And I have other sheep that are not of this fold. I must bring them also, and they will listen to my voice. Thus, there will be one flock, one shepherd. For this reason, the Father loves me, because I lay down my life that I may take it up again. No one takes it from me, but I lay it down of my own accord. I have authority to lay it down, and I have authority to take it up again. This charge I have received from my Father."

"Amen," the pastor concluded as he closed the Bible.

The pastor then descended from the pulpit and met privately with the teens and I in the front row of the sheepfold.

***

Later that day, I was back on duty at the park when I heard a woman scream. I looked up in time to see a man snatch the lady's purse and run off toward the edge of the park. The dog heard the scream too and jumped up from beneath a bench.

I threw down my tools and began to run after the purse snatcher. The dog was already in pursuit. I will never know how, but I soon found myself passing the hurried hound and tackling the thief.

I rolled the robber over on his back and pounced on top of him, the dog circling us with its growling gnashing teeth. He appeared to be some kind of wretched wino.

"Okay, okay, I give up! I don't want the purse! Please don't hurt me!" he pathetically pleaded.

I looked down at his anguished face and I suddenly froze...

I recognized the bandit below me...
I remembered the brigand beneath me...
Yes, I recalled this mugger's mug!

"I know you!" I spat.

"Let me go!" he responded. "What's wrong with you anyway?!"

"It's you!" I accused, raising my fist. "I know it's you!"

"Are you some kinda psycho or something?!" he squealed. "Let me up!"

"I remember now!" I yelled, reeling my arm and fist back, ready to strike.

"You don't know me!" he beseeched. "Just take the stupid purse and leave me alone!"

I wailed: "I was changing my tire that night! You grabbed the tire iron and smashed me in the head with it!"

"Oh, god!" he screamed to the heavens. "Please don't kill me!"

The fist I had raised in anger fell limp to my side.

"I'm not going to kill you," I said in a calmer voice.

"Thank you, Mister," he responded. "Please forgive me. I didn't mean to hit you that hard."

Still on top of him, I asked, "Do you have my wallet?"

"No, sir," he cried. "I threw it away. I - I just kept the cash."

"Where's my car?" I continued.

"I left it where it was," he confessed, "at that small market on Eighth. It probably got towed."

"Do you remember what kind of car it was?"

"What?"

The dog snapped viciously at his ears.

I clenched my teeth and repeated, "I said, do you remember what kind of car it was?!"

"I'm not sure," he said. "Some kind of light-colored sedan...Maybe a Toyota, but I can't say for sure."

I got off the crook and told the dog to quiet down. Ironically, I don't know if I would've had the ability to forgive the man for what he'd done, if he hadn't struck me that night.

I promptly returned the purse to its owner and I recognized her too.

"Here's your purse, ma'am," I said as I handed it over.

"Oh, thank you, kind sir!" the businesswoman excitedly exclaimed. "I wish there were more men like you! How can I re-pay you? Do you need any cash?"

I just smiled at her and replied, "The time to help me was that morning when we met at the bus stop."

Her face turned pale as she stammered, "Bus stop?"

***

The dog and I took a walk to Eighth Street.

Accordingly, I entered the Eighth Street Market, while the dog obediently waited outside.

The market was modest, the uptight owner not so much.

"Excuse me," I announced as I approached the counter. "My car broke down outside your market a few days ago. Can you tell me what may have happened to it?"

"Can you tell me why you abandoned it?" she challenged.

"Well, I didn't really abandon it," I corrected her choice of words. "I was attacked by a thug while I was changing a tire."

"I guess that explains all the blood I had to clean up off the sidewalk."

I cringed and unconsciously rubbed my head.

"Obviously, I managed to walk away, at least I think I did," I admitted. "But I don't remember much else about that night."

"Well, I want you to know that I did wait a while for the owner to return before I called the towing company," she explained.

"I appreciate that," I said.

"And you were in a No Parking Zone," she added.

"I didn't realize that," I apologized for no reason. "But I'm not questioning your decision to call a tow truck."

"Then why are you here?" she inquired. "I doubt it's for the fresh produce we offer every day."

I politely looked around at the stocked shelves and agreed, "You have a fine selection, I see."

"Thank you for noticing, sir."

I paused and smiled, then added, "So, maybe you could tell me what tow company you called."

"The apples are fresh off the truck this morning."

"I'm sure they are," I played along. "But I need to find my car. Certainly, you remember what towing company you called."

"Towing company?"

"Yes, Miss, which one did you call to take my vehicle?"

"Well, the same one I always call!" she replied.

"And that company is…?"

"Because of that No Parking Zone, I'm calling for tows all the time."

"Ma'am, is there a reason you won't tell me the name of the company?"

"Of course not!" she answered like she was offended. "It's Monroe Towing. It's the closest one to my store, so I use them mostly."

"Exactly how close to the store is it, if you don't mind me asking?"

"It's just a couple blocks up Eighth," she explained, "then turn left on Monroe Avenue."

"Thank you."

"I figure it's called Monroe Towing because they're located on Monroe Avenue," she added.

"Like I said," I likely said. "Thank you. You've been very helpful."

"Are you sure you don't want to grab any fresh apples or oranges for your trip to the tow yard?"

"No thank you, I'm a little short on funds right now," I admitted. "But maybe you could help me with the color or model."

"Of the apples?"

"No," I expounded, "the color or model of the car that was towed."

She raised an eyebrow and replied, "You don't know the color or model of your own car?"

"Young lady," I concluded. "After I got struck on the head with the tire iron, I couldn't even remember my own name."

"Oh, sorry," she realized. "I didn't realize it was that bad. Your car was a white Toyota Camry."

"God bless you, Miss," I answered. "I just hope the tow company still has it on the lot!"

"Hey, no problemo," she colloquialized with a sympathetic smile. "Please grab a fresh apple on your way out. It's on the house!"

***

The dog and I took a walk farther up Eighth Street, until we reached Monroe Avenue.

"It shouldn't be too much farther, boy," I said. "I see Monroe Avenue just ahead."

The dog could not properly respond, because it was joyfully carrying my complimentary apple in its jowls.

The dog and I turned left at the corner and hiked until we reached the site of a large junkyard. As I approached the business office, I left the dog outside to enjoy the fruit of our labor.

Upon entering the lobby, I observed a stocky older gentleman at the counter, smoking a cigar and typing with single-digits on a plastic-covered keyboard.

The grumpy-looking man glanced up from his dusty desktop computer screen and asked me, "What d'ya need?"

"Ah, yes," I answered politely. "I was hoping you could help me."

He looked back at the screen and mumbled, "How's that?"

"Well, a few days ago, the market on Eighth Street called you to tow away a white Camry."

"So?" he belligerently bellowed.

"So... that car belongs to me."

He looked back at me and surmised, "So, you've come to pay the tow fee?"

"Well, not necessarily," I admitted after an uncomfortable pause.

He leaned toward me over the counter and informed me, "Then I can't help you."

"But you don't understand..." I tried to explain.

A landline telephone on the counter rang and the miserable man picked up the receiver. "Excuse me," he cut me off.

He then poked a couple keys on the keyboard and

spoke into the receiver. "Monroe Towing, how may I help you?... Yes, we're located on Monroe Avenue... Sorry to hear that... I hope there were no injuries... Yes, we know where that is... We can certainly get over there, but all our trucks are busy at present... It might be an hour before we can reach you, is that okay?... Yes, we'll do our best to get there as soon as possible, ma'am... Bye."

The malicious man hung up the phone and reached into his pocket for his cellphone.

"As I was saying," I began saying.

The disingenuous gent ignored me as he put the cellphone up to his ear.

"Yeah, Jack," he spoke into the phone. "A lady just called in from an accident on Fifth and Jefferson. What would be your E.T.A., if you don't already have a vehicle in tow?... Yeah, you can finish your meal. There's no rush... I told her about an hour, but she'll just have to wait until you get there... Beggars can't be choosers... Ha!... Thanks... Bye."

I stood by with a shocked look on my face, at least I assume I appeared shocked. The man put his cell back in his pocket and began typing again.

I cleared my throat to attain his attention.

The rude dude looked up from the computer screen and commented, "You still here?"

"Well, yeah, I mean, I think you have my car somewhere on your lot."

"Like I said, buddy, no fee, no car, no exceptions," he quoted his policy. "Now if you'll excuse me, I have work to do."

"Can I at least explain to you what's going on with the car?"

The belabored bully rolled his eyes and reluctantly agreed, "Okay, but make it quick, 'cause I don't got all day."

"All right, a few nights ago I got a flat tire on Eighth Street and when I started to fix the flat, I got jumped by a hoodlum. He cracked my skull with a tire iron and took everything I had. Somehow, I ended up underneath a bridge with a bunch of homeless people. One of them tried to steal my boots. Anyway, I soon realized that I had amnesia and couldn't remember who I was or even where I was. I tried asking some folks, but a cop picked me up for panhandling and I was tossed in a cell with a couple of inmates who thought I wanted to fight. The next day, the judge threw me out into the street because she thought I was trying to scam the government. Then I got pushed in a fountain."

"I thought I told you to keep it short, buddy," he interrupted.

"I'm trying," I urged. "I just want you to know what I've been going through..."

"Is this some kind of a joke?" he asked. "Are you secretly filming me for a viral video prank or something? You know, like Tick Tock Instant Camera Candid Gram?"

"What?" I wondered. "No! I'm being serious and I'm hoping you can show me a little empathy for my dire situation."

He sighed and said, "Okay, bud, what is it you want me to do?"

"Can you at least look up the VIN on the white Toyota Camry that was recently towed here?"

"No, I cannot," he answered with a mischievous grin.

"Excuse me?"

"You heard me," he responded with an even more mischievous smirk. "Now be on your way and have a nice day."

"What?... Why?... Why can't you do that for me?" I questioned.

"Because I don't know you from Adam," he concluded. "You don't have any I.D., but you want me to search the D.M.V. database to find the owner of a car."

"Yes," I argued. "Considering my current plight, that is exactly what I'd like you to do."

"Well, you can fur-git it!" he raised his voice. "How do I know you don't work for the government and you're testing me to see if I'd hand out confidential registration information?"

"Seriously?" I dead panned.

"Yes, seriously!" he shot back. "Now git your sorry self outta my place of business before I call the cops!"

"Go ahead and call the cops," I challenged as I retreated. "I'll be waiting outside. Maybe they'll help me."

"Yeah," he called after me. "And maybe they will help you into a squad car and then throw you back in the slammer where you belong!"

After I left the building, I heard the angry man locking the door from inside. He also flagrantly flipped over a sign on the glass to read CLOSED.

I kneeled to the dog and sadly informed him, "I think I may have worn out my welcome here."

I saw that the dog had no clue what I was saying, so I gently patted his head and added, "Did you eat that whole apple, core and all?"

The dog barked in response.

I stood up and began walking past the closed office, eventually reaching a fenced-in lot with a lot of cars. The dog followed me as I patrolled the perimeter, peering through the chain links at the vanquished vehicles within.

"Hey, boy!" I excitedly announced. "I think I see it! A white Camry, just inside the fence!"

The dog picked up on my excitement and began enthusiastically jumping and barking.

"I wish I could just get in there," I said, taking a quick glance around me. "I wish I could just sit in that car for a few minutes... Maybe it would all come back to me!"

I boldly put my fingers inside links above my head and planted the toe of my boot into a link just above my other knee. But as soon as I hoisted myself up onto the fence, I heard bloodcurdling barking – and it sure wasn't coming from my dog.

A crazed junkyard dog slammed its mangy head directly into the inside of the fence and tried biting me as I hung on the opposite side. Both my dog and I yelped in terror as we ran away from the fence.

We didn't slow down until we reached a residential neighborhood. Out of breath and out of ideas, I dejectedly trudged along the lovely lawns and sculpted shrubs of suburbia. Children were riding skates and scooters on the secluded sidewalks, while their parents cleaned their cars on sud-soaked driveways.

I strolled past a paper sign stapled to a pole. I strolled past another. But when I came to a third, I stopped and read the sign. I sincerely wished I hadn't.

The sign had a photocopied image of a German shepherd and the word LOST.

I shook my head and looked down at the dog. "Is this you?" I asked in utter disbelief.

I had just lost my car and now I may lose my dog?

I wanted so much to just run through the neighborhood and rip down every sign I could find.

But would that be fair to the dog? I asked myself. I realized that this dog had helped me (saved my life!) and the least I could do was discover if he belonged to the family that had posted the posters.

I read the address on the sign and called out, "Come on, boy, we need to find one-eleven Elm Street."

It turns out we were already on Elm Street and very close to 111.

We were soon standing in the driveway of the home. No one was outside, so I approached the front door and knocked. With tears streaming down my cheeks, I fell to the ground and hugged the whimpering dog.

"I hope it's not you, boy," I cried. "But we have to check."

Suddenly, a pre-teen girl burst through the front door and screamed, "Mommy, mommy! Daddy brought our dog home!"

My baby girl jumped on top of me and I raised my arms to the sky, and I thanked God for my deliverance. Yes, I was home. I was finally home!

EPILOGUE

I remember waking up on a bed with a splitting headache and some crazy-looking gal trying to steal my boots.

Okay, the gal was my wife, and she was only removing my boots after I had passed out in exhaustion on top of our bed.

Before I fell back asleep, I asked her again to tell me who I was, and she again told me, "Darling, you're a writer."

Wow, I guess I was a poet and didn't know it!

PHOTOS FROM THE MOVIE

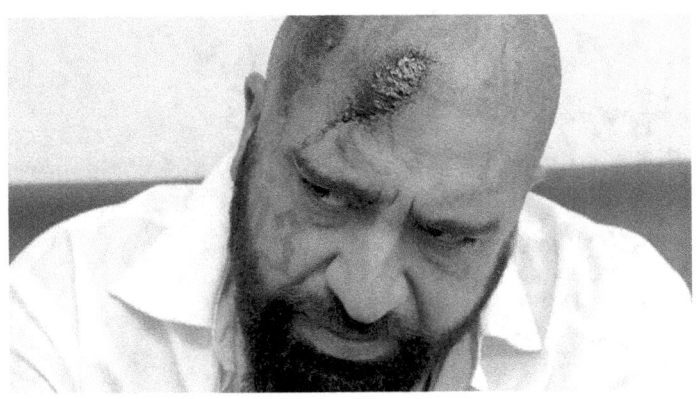

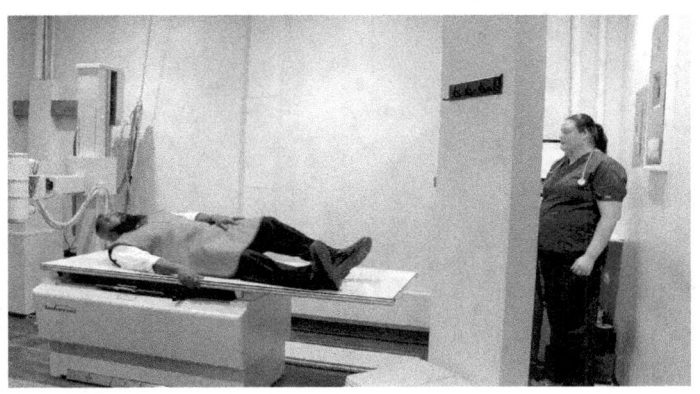

THE ORIGINAL SCREENPLAY

<u>Godsend</u>

by
Rich Bottles Jr.

Fade In:

SCENE 01 - EXT. DAY. CITY RUSH HOUR

Various establishing shots of a busy city during morning
rush hour, like traffic jams, horns blowing, hurrying
pedestrians, etc. The final shot should be that of a bridge.

SCENE 02 - EXT. DAY. BENEATH A BRIDGE

An unseen world of homeless people is revealed by the
camera. Some are huddled together. Some are eating food from
a can. Some are hidden in makeshift tents. The final shot is
of an old disheveled homeless man crawling up to a lifeless
man and attempting to remove the lifeless man's shoes/boots.
The lifeless man's name is John and he is dressed in a dirty
business suit.

The unusual activity at his feet causes John to stir and
awaken.

                    JOHN
              (shaken and confused)
          Hey! What are doing? Leave me
          alone!

John kicks at the old disheveled man, who had been tugging
at one of John's untied shoes/boots.

                    OLD DISHEVELED MAN
              (backing away from John)
          Sorry, Mister... I swear I thought
          you was dead.

                    JOHN
          Just get away from me!

The old disheveled man hastily crawls away as John begins to
re-tie his shoes/boots. Once his shoes/boots are tied, he
begins to look at his surroundings and appears extremely
confused.

                    JOHN (CONT'D)
              (panicked)
          Where am I?! Who are you people?!
          What have you done to me?!

John attempts to stand up, but is wobbly and dizzy, so he
sits back down. He grimaces and grabs the back of his head.
His fingers feel around his head until he finds a large bump
or welt. He then looks at his hand to see if there's any
blood.

                    JOHN (CONT'D)
              (to himself)
          My head. What's wrong with my
          head? Oh, god it hurts.

John leans back and appears to pass out again. Fades to
black...

[Opening Credits Roll]

Fade in:

Light then returns and the camera is in John's POV, at first
blurred and then slowly focusing on a homeless woman leaning
over him.

> HOMELESS WOMAN
> (worried)
> Are you okay, fella? You don't
> look so good. I brought you some
> water. I ain't even opened the
> bottle yet. You wanna drink?

> JOHN
> A drink?

> HOMELESS WOMAN
> (opening the water bottle)
> Yes, a drink. You want me to hold
> it to yer mouth?

> JOHN
> Please, yes, I need water. I don't
> feel well.

The homeless woman holds the plastic bottle to John's mouth
and he begins to drink. He drinks most of the bottle.

> HOMELESS WOMAN
> (pulling back the bottle
> when John stops drinking)
> I guess you was thirsty!

> JOHN
> Thank you. I needed that.

> HOMELESS WOMAN
> Yer welcome. We all need some help
> ever now n' agin.

> JOHN
> Where am I? Please tell me where I
> am.

"Hurry, before I come to my senses or change my mind. The woman needs some new manure for her column."

The man tried to keep from laughing, but finally he burst out, his deep voice vibrating through the barn.

"All right, ma'am. Just don't get me fired."

"Never," she said. "Now I'll go back into the house and continue to be a good girl, even though everyone has decided I'm bad."

CHAPTER 16

*A*fter Hayden's meeting, he walked over to see his good friend Levi at his hotel. He'd read his mother's brutal society column. The woman was an evil witch, and one day, someone was going to end her nasty, mean columns.

He'd already had his secretary fire off a letter to the editor of the paper. When would they wise up and fire the woman?

When he reached his friend's office, his secretary waved him in. "He's expecting you."

Without responding, Hayden walked in.

"I knew you would come see me today. I've already spoken to her."

He sank down in the chair. "Thank you."

That wasn't the entire reason he was there to see his friend, but it was one thing he wanted to speak to him about.

"How do you live with her?"

Levi laughed. "Sometimes it's not easy."

Not knowing how to start the conversation, he just blurted out what was on his mind. "I'm considering proposing to Rose."

Levi's head jerked at the news. "It seems early. Are you certain?"

"It's the only way we can rid ourselves of her father and his congregation. And then I would take my wife to New York to audition for the opera there."

Levi smiled. "Wow, she is determined."

"It's her dream and if I want Rose, then I have to accept her wishes and her dreams."

His friend grinned. "True."

"If I propose to her, will you be my best man at our very impromptu, secretive wedding?"

He'd spoken to his mother this morning and told her that he was thinking of proposing. She'd been so excited, but he also worried about his father's reaction.

"Of course. It would be an honor," Levi said. "But why haven't you proposed yet? What's holding you back."

Yes, he knew that he loved Rose, but there was her family situation. Would they have to deal with this all their lives? But the main reason holding him back was Rose.

"I'm just not certain she loves me. As much as I love her and I recognize she has a dream, is it wrong for me to want to be just as important as her desire to be an opera singer. I'm not willing to be in second place, though I will help her achieve her dream."

All night he had wondered if she would ever put him first. Tell him that she loves him and want to make him happy. For now, he was willing to accept she didn't love him, but he couldn't go through life not receiving her love.

With a nod, Levi agreed. "How will you know that she loves you?"

That was the million dollar question. Was he willing to gamble on her falling for him?

"It's a risk. Right now, she's being honest and telling me she cares for me, but she's never said she loves me. What if I marry her and she never falls in love with me? What If I'm never more important than her singing opera?"

For a moment, his friend sat listening, not responding and Hayden knew he was right to worry. And yet, he also realized that he loved Rose and had from the moment he heard her singing in the saloon. It was like her voice wrapped around his body and entered his heart.

"You're right to be concerned. What if she is only marrying you to get away from her father's choice for husband?"

He didn't think that was what she was doing, but could he be so blinded by his love for her not to be seeing clearly?

Hayden nodded. "Last night, the only way we escaped was by going up to the roof and crossing several and coming out at O'Hara's. When we reached the alley, we barely made it into the carriage."

Levi's face became alarmed.

"This is getting dangerous. Her father is going to do everything to capture her and bring her home," Levi said. "I can see why you're considering marriage. It's the only way to stop him."

That's the conclusion that Hayden had arrived at. If they were married, he couldn't take her and make her marry anyone else, without killing him.

"Yes, but is this marriage right for me?"

"Only you can decide that," Levi said.

Hayden knew it was a decision that could either make his life wonderful or devastate him. And his friend was wise for not giving him the answer. Only he could decide if this was right for him.

"What about you and Sadie? How are your wedding plans coming along?"

Levi grinned. "We're going to announce the date very soon. A fall wedding."

"Congratulations. She'll make you very happy."

The man grinned. "Yes, I think so."

They were silent for a moment and then Hayden said softly, "If I send you a message to come to my parents' house, be sure to bring Sadie and even Tessa if you can. I'm sure that Rose would love to have her friends at the ceremony."

"Levi!" a female voice screamed.

"Oh no, you're going to witness one of my mother's melt downs. Don't ever tell Sadie about these or she will never marry me," Levi said, shaking his head and rising from his chair.

Just then his mother Betty Griffin, a woman that Hayden despised, rushed into the room, her face red, her eyes wide with anger. "Look what she sent me."

The smell hit them both at the same time and they reeled back. "What is that?"

"It's horse manure. She compared my column to horse manure."

Suddenly, Hayden started laughing. "Rose sent you horse manure?"

"Yes," Mrs. Griffin snarled, turning to him and shoving the box at him. "Your Rose did not appreciate my column and compared it to horse shit."

While he knew he shouldn't be, he was proud of how Rose had stood up to the woman. He'd hid the paper this morning, hoping she wouldn't find it, but apparently she had. And she had extracted her revenge.

"Mrs. Griffin, surely there must be better news you could report other than trying to harm young women. And frankly, I completely agree with Rose. Your column is nothing but horse manure."

The woman's mouth dropped open and she glared at him.

He turned to Levi. "Thanks for listening. I'll be in touch."

With that, Hayden walked out of his friend's office, laughing all the way. A retaliatory streak of fire resided in the woman he loved and he admired it.

When he reached the door out of the hotel, the local mean girls were just entering.

"Hayden," Nellie Robinson called. She walked over to him and laid her hand on his arm.

The woman was a gold digger if he'd ever met one. And that included her friends, Helen Davis and Carrie Miller. A nastier trio, he'd never met.

"Good afternoon, Nellie, ladies," he said.

"We're about to have lunch, you're welcome to join us," Nellie said, moving in closer to him.

He took a step back. "Thank you, but I've got an appointment this afternoon."

"Oh. Will you be attending the Fall Festival Ball?" Carrie asked.

"No, ladies, probably not," he said, thinking he probably would be in New York. Suddenly he realized he'd already made his decision. If he was thinking ahead, he knew he wanted to marry Rose. He loved her, and no matter what, it was what his heart wanted.

What was he waiting for?

"Ladies, it was lovely to see you, but I must be going. Take care," he said and walked away.

Speaking with Levi had cleared his mind of what his heart already knew. He loved Rose and would marry her hoping she would eventually love him.

The time had come for him to propose.

CHAPTER 17

*S*teward Hayden Lee wanted only the best for his son. After all, he was his only son, and while the man knew how to choose a lovely woman, as his father, he wanted more. He expected more from a woman for his son.

Not that horrid preacher's daughter. The girl was stunning and she could sing like an angel, but she didn't have a dowry or social status or anything else that his son needed.

It was time to consider finding a woman on his own. But who?

Martin Davis had a beautiful daughter named Helen. A blonde with blue eyes and a shapely figure. Her father a banker, she must surely come with a dowry, not that they needed her money, but her standing in society would be good for his son.

Steward walked out of his home and down the street to the bank. Maybe it was time the two of them had a chat about their children.

As he entered the building, he couldn't help but smile. The bank was nothing compared to his office for the railroad.

A few moments later, he was sitting in a comfortable chair in front of Martin.

"Are you needing a loan," Martin said to him with a grin, knowing that he did not need the bank's money.

"No, I'm needing a wife for my son," he told the man whose brows rose, a grin spreading across his face.

"And my daughter needs a husband," he said. "That girl spends way too much time with Nellie Robinson, the mayor's daughter."

This sounded good.

"Your daughter, I think, would be perfect for my son. Currently he's involved with a woman who is beautiful but not for him."

The bank manager grinned. "How can we introduce the two of them?"

"How about tomorrow night at dinner at the Griffin Hotel? I'll insist that my son attend and tell him it's a business engagement. Which it could be," Steward said with a smile.

"And I'll insist that Helen attend dinner with me," he said.

The two men stood and shook hands.

"Let's hope this works out for us both," he said.

"Yes, to a husband for my daughter and a wife for your son," the banker replied. "After they're engaged, we'll smoke some of my Cuban cigars to celebrate."

"It's a plan," Steward said as he turned to leave.

CHAPTER 18

*H*ayden received an urgent message from his father saying to meet him at the Griffin Hotel for dinner tonight.

All he wanted to do was return home and be with Rose. To make certain she was safe, but instead, he was on his way to the Griffin Hotel. At least he had gotten out of having lunch with Nellie and her friends.

As he walked into the hotel, he wanted to make this as quick as possible since he did not want to tarry long from Rose's side.

After last night's fiasco at the saloon, they had made the difficult decision that she would no longer sing there. And that saddened both her and him because he enjoyed listening to her sing.

As he walked into the hotel, he saw his father waiting for him. He hurried over to his side.

"Son, so good of you to come," he said.

"What's so urgent that we couldn't talk later?"

"Come with me," his father said. "I have such a lovely surprise for you."

A trickle of alarm scurried up his spine. Most of the time, his father's surprises were more work.

As they reached a table, he saw Martin Davis, the banker, and his daughter Helen sitting there waiting for them. What had his father done?

Everyone rose when they approached the table.

"You know Martin Davis, son. How about his lovely daughter Helen? Do you know her?"

"Yes, we've met," he said, glancing at his father. What was he up to?

They all sat at the table. An awkward silence hung about as they settled in.

"Hayden, weren't you here this morning?"

"Yes, I came to speak to my friend Levi, who owns the hotel. You were with Nellie Robinson and Carrie Miller."

"We had lunch here," she said smiling. "How did your meeting go?"

"Very well, thank you," he said. "Not long after that I received an urgent message from my father about dinner tonight."

The two men looked nervous. Were they trying to introduce him to Helen with the hope that they would become interested in one another?

"Father, what was so urgent about tonight?"

"Mr. Davis and I thought that you might want to know more about what the bank has to offer our company."

That was about a lame an excuse as he'd ever heard.

For the next five minutes, they listened to Martin tell him all about their bank and the different services they offered. Since he was soon leaving for New York and knew the company had been banking with another bank since before he was born, he doubted that his father was interested in changing.

"Are you still seeing Rose Tuttle? Even with her father searching the town for her?" Helen asked him.

"Yes," he said. "I plan to ask for her hand in marriage very soon."

A gasp came from the banker and with a quick glance at his father, he watched him close his eyes and shake his head.

Most definitely this was a setup for him to meet Helen, fall madly in love with her and offer for her hand in marriage.

And hell no, it wasn't going to happen.

"Excuse me, folks," he said standing. He took his father by the elbow and led him outside.

"What the hell are you doing?"

"I'm trying to find you a wife with a good social standing, a dowry, and who doesn't have a crazy family."

"Well, good luck with that. I'm leaving. Never would I be interested in Helen Davis, even if she were the last woman on earth. She and Nellie Robinson are two of the meanest girls in Fort Worth."

They were standing out in the hallway talking and would move as people passed them by.

"Then I'll keep trying," his father said.

"And I said no. I'm not interested. I've found the woman I intend to marry and if you had not interrupted me tonight, I would have asked her."

His father shook his head vehemently. "Wait and let me try to find someone else."

Did he not understand? Rose was who he wanted to marry.

                    HOMELESS WOMAN
          Well, yer under the Second Avenue
          bridge. Don't you remember how you
          got here?

                    JOHN
               (still confused)
          No, I don't remember. I'm having
          trouble remembering anything... I
          think I hurt my head.

                    HOMELESS WOMAN
          You must-ah hurt yer head
          somethin' fierce, 'cause folks
          dressed as nice as you don't
          usually hang out under this
          bridge.

John glances down at his clothes and fingers his loosened
necktie.

                    JOHN
          Say, do you think you could help
          me to my feet? I don't know if I
          can stand on my own.

                    HOMELESS WOMAN
               (standing up)
          I kin sure try. Here, take hold of
          my hand.

John reaches his hand up to grasp the homeless woman's hand
and slowly uses her as leverage in order to stand up.

                    JOHN
          I made it! But my head's still
          killing me.

                    HOMELESS WOMAN
          You think you can stand now?

                    JOHN
               (lets go of the woman's
                hand)
          Yes, I think I can even walk.

                    HOMELESS WOMAN
          Well, you be careful and take it
          easy, ya hear?

                    JOHN
               (a bit shaky)
          Yes, yes, I'll be careful. Thank
          you again for helping me.

John begins to slowly walk away.

HOMELESS WOMAN
Sure thing... By the way, what's
yer name?

John glances back at the homeless woman.

JOHN
(pauses to contemplate, then
shakes his head in dismay)
Heck if I know.

SCENE 03 - EXT. DAY. CITY SIDEWALK

John is seen stumbling along a sidewalk, looking around
desperately to see if he recognizes anything or anyone.
Hurried pedestrians bump into him, even though he tries to
avoid their stride. It's difficult for John to make eye
contact with anyone, but when he does, he pleads with a
businessman.

> JOHN
> (trying to get in front of a
> businessman)
> Sir, please... Can you tell me
> where I am?!

> BUSINESSMAN
> (impatiently)
> Get out of my way, bum! I have no
> spare change!

> JOHN
> (as the businessman walks
> past him)
> But I'm not asking for change...

John continues to walk the crowded sidewalk. The camera
gives brief glimpses of pedestrian faces, all very stern as
if they are late for work. Everyone ignores John as though
he doesn't exist.

> JOHN (CONT'D)
> (desperately)
> Please! Would somebody tell me
> where I am?

No one responds to John's plea, but continue to walk around
him like he is some kind of obstacle.

John stumbles upon a bus stop on a corner. He sees people
standing still, waiting for a bus. He lightly grabs a
miscellaneous woman's arm to get her attention.

> JOHN (CONT'D)
> (trying to be calm)
> Please, ma'am, can you please tell
> me where I am?

The miscellaneous woman is startled and shakes her arm loose
from John's grasp. She screams.

> MISCELLANEOUS WOMAN
> (yelling)
> Let go of me!

The miscellaneous woman's scream attracts the attention of a policeman/beat cop across the street. The beat cop dashes across the street to the bus stop.

                    BEAT COP
                (to the woman)
            What's going on here? What's the
            problem?

                    MISCELLANEOUS WOMAN
                (nodding toward John)
            This vagrant just tried to attack
            me!

                    BEAT COP
                (turning his attention to
                John)
            Is that right, fella?

                    JOHN
                (scared and stuttering)
            N-no sir, officer sir, I just
            wanted to ask her a question...

                    MISCELLANEOUS WOMAN
            He grabbed onto my arm, officer,
            and wouldn't let go!

                    BEAT COP
                (to John)
            Did you grab this woman's arm?

                    JOHN
            I-I didn't mean to, I just touched
            her arm to get her attention,
            because...

                    BEAT COP
                (interrupting John)
            You need to keep your filthy hands
            to yourself, you hear me?

                    JOHN
            Ah, yes. Yes, sir.

                    BEAT COP
            And we have ordinances in the town
            against panhandling.

                    JOHN
                (slowly)
            And what town would this be?

                    BEAT COP
            Excuse me?

> JOHN
> (louder)
> What town is this? I need to know
> what city I am in.

> BEAT COP
> (getting angry)
> Are you trying to be funny?

> JOHN
> No, no, I'm serious...

The beat cop quickly removes his baton from his utility belt.

> BEAT COP
> (raising the baton)
> Welcome to the city of hard
> knocks!

The beat cop swings the baton and hits John on the head. John yelps and crumples to the cement. The beat cop returns the baton to his utility belt.

A bus pulls up to the bus stop and passengers begin boarding. The miscellaneous woman steps over-top of John in order to get on the bus.

> MISCELLANEOUS WOMAN
> Thank you, officer.

> BEAT COP
> (tipping his cap and
> smiling)
> My pleasure, madam.

As the bus pulls away, the beat cop pulls out a hand-held radio or cell phone device and speaks into it.

> BEAT COP (CONT'D)
> Yeah, dispatch, this is
> Nine-Oh-Two-Nine-One, can you send
> a wagon over to Second and Main?

SCENE 04 - INT. DAY. LARGE JAIL CELL

When John wakes up this time, he is inside a precinct jail
cell with some other inmates. He is sitting on the floor
with his back against the wall. He immediately grabs his
aching head and moans. An inmate leaning against the
opposite wall hears John.

>   FIRST INMATE
>   Well, lookie who's awake... Good
>   morning, er, afternoon, Mister
>   Fancypants.

The other inmates in the cell chuckle.

John looks up, his face still distraught, as he surveys his
new surroundings.

>   JOHN
>   Wah-what?

>   FIRST INMATE
>   (approaching John)
>   I said, good afternoon,
>   Fancypants. Ain't you got no
>   manners?

>   JOHN
>   (still confused)
>   Manners? Who are you anyway?

First inmate lightly kicks/nudges at John's leg.

>   FIRST INMATE
>   Nunya bidness who I is! We wanna
>   know what you did to git in here!

>   JOHN
>   (glaring at first inmate)
>   I don't know how I got here or who
>   put me in here.

>   FIRST INMATE
>   Is that right?

>   JOHN
>   Who put me in this cell?

                    FIRST INMATE
          You was drugged in by one-ah the
          pigs!

                    JOHN
          For what?

John slowly rises to his feet by using the wall as leverage.
He is now face-to-face with first inmate.

                    FIRST INMATE
                  (in John's face)
          That's what we wanna know...

                    FIRST INMATE (CONT'D)
                  (turns his head toward the
                  other inmates)
          ... ain't that right, boys?

                    SECOND INMATE
          Yeah, yeah, we see yer tats, but
          you ain't wearin' no colors.

                    JOHN
          I told you I don't remember
          anything.

                    FIRST INMATE
                  (in John's face)
          That's typical.

                    JOHN
          Typical? Typical of what?

The second and third inmates approach John.

                    THIRD INMATE
                  (getting in close to John)
          Typical response of a gang-
          banger.

                    JOHN
                  (getting frightened)
          Gang-banger? I'm no gang-banger.

                    FIRST INMATE
          You muss be, 'cause yer so scared
          without yer homies to protect you.

                    SECOND INMATE
          Yeah, scared.

                    THIRD INMATE
          So tell us what you did... I
          smacked my wife in the mouth for
          back-talking.

                    FIRST INMATE
          I robbed a store.

                    SECOND INMATE
          I was drunk and dressed orderly.

All three inmates are now staring at John.

                    JOHN
               (stuttering)
          S-sorry, g-guys, but all I
          remember is wondering the streets
          and asking for help because I was
          injured...

                    FIRST INMATE
          Lyin' gang-banger! Git him boys!

The inmates surround John and begin throwing punches, but
instinct takes over and John begins to fight back. Although
he gets caught with a couple punches, including one square
on the jaw, one-by-one John knocks all three inmates to the
cell floor.

SCENE 05 - INT. DAY. MAKESHIFT COURTROOM

John is seated at a folding table in a nondescript room. A
television screen is hanging on the wall in front of him,
the screen is staticky. A small camera is mounted on the
wall above the TV. John's face is covered in dried blood.

A smartly-dressed young man/woman with a briefcase enters
the room and sits down at the table beside John. John looks
over at the person. The person is a public defender.

                    PUBLIC DEFENDER
          Hey, man, what happened to you?

The public defender snaps open his/her briefcase and begins
fingering through some papers.

                    JOHN
                (mumbling)
          I had a disagreement with some
          other inmates.

The public defender continues to finger through papers.

                    PUBLIC DEFENDER
                (distracted)
          Sorry, what did you say?

                    JOHN
                (trying to talk through the
                pain)
          I got beat up.

                    PUBLIC DEFENDER
                (looks toward John)
          Beat up, huh? That's pretty
          obvious.

                    JOHN
                (reaching a hand to his
                chin)
          I think my jaw might be broken.

                    PUBLIC DEFENDER
          Oh! That's too bad. Because we're
          going to be talking to the judge
          in a minute and you're going to
          have to speak up so he can hear
          you.

                    JOHN
          Who are you?

                    PUBLIC DEFENDER
                (reaching his/her hand over
                toward John)
            My bad... I guess I failed to
            introduce myself. I'm your
            designated public defender.

                    JOHN
                (briefly shakes the public
                defender's hand)
            And do you have a name?

                    PUBLIC DEFENDER
                (taking his hand back)
            That's not important. You just
            need some kind of token
            representation, because that's how
            the justice system works.

The public defender is seen reaching into the briefcase to
retrieve a bottle of hand sanitizer.

                    JOHN
            I don't either.

                    PUBLIC DEFENDER
                (rubbing the sanitizer into
                his/her hands)
            You don't what?

                    JOHN
            I don't have a name.

                    PUBLIC DEFENDER
                (picking up a piece of
                paper)
            A name? Of course you do... It's
            right here... John?

                    JOHN
            John?

                    PUBLIC DEFENDER
                (reading the paper)
            Yeah, John... John Doe...

                    JOHN
            My name is John Doe?

                    PUBLIC DEFENDER
                (looking back toward John)
            Well, that's obviously not your
            real name.

JOHN

Obviously.

PUBLIC DEFENDER
(grabs a pen from the
briefcase and places his/her
piece of paper on the table)
They must have just booked you
under the name John Doe because
you were unresponsive.

JOHN

Yes, I was. I was very
unresponsive.

PUBLIC DEFENDER
(looking down at the paper,
ready to write)
Right. So if I could just get your
full name for the case file...

JOHN

I don't know.

PUBLIC DEFENDER
(looks toward John)
You don't know whether you want to
give me your full name?

JOHN

No, I don't know what my name is.

PUBLIC DEFENDER
Very funny, but this is no time
for games.

JOHN

I'm telling you, I don't remember.
I think I got hit on the head and
it jarred my memory or something.

PUBLIC DEFENDER
Well, that's not good.

JOHN

I agree.

PUBLIC DEFENDER
The judge is going to want to know
who you are.

                    JOHN
Not as much as I want to know.

                PUBLIC DEFENDER
            (checks his/her wristwatch)
You'd be surprised... Listen, we
haven't got much time and we need
to go over the charges.

                    JOHN
Okay, tell me what I did.

                PUBLIC DEFENDER
            (reading the paper)
What you did... Okay, here are the
charges from the arresting
officer... Aggressive Panhandling
and Assault.

                    JOHN
That doesn't sound right.

                PUBLIC DEFENDER
            (looking back at John)
And it probably isn't right,
because I know this officer tends
to exaggerate when it comes to
filing charges.

                    JOHN
Okay, so I plead innocent, right?

                PUBLIC DEFENDER
Of course not. Don't be silly.
You're going to plead guilty as
charged.

                    JOHN
            (surprised)
What?

                PUBLIC DEFENDER
You heard me. You're going to
plead guilty. I'm going to tell
the judge it's your first offense.
And the judge is going to let you
walk out of here.

                    JOHN
But I'm innocent... At least I
think I am.

                    PUBLIC DEFENDER
          That's the problem. You can't
          prove it.

                    JOHN
          But the defendant shouldn't have
          to prove his innocence.

                    PUBLIC DEFENDER
                  (laughs)
          You've been watching too much TV,
          Mister Doe.

                    JOHN
          Whatever... I may not remember my
          name, but I think I know how the
          justice system is supposed to
          work.

                    PUBLIC DEFENDER
                  (annoyed)
          Not in this jurisdiction you
          don't. If you plead not guilty,
          the judge is going to call in the
          arresting officer to testify. The
          officer will probably be angry and
          will add on new charges, which the
          judge will believe every word.

                    JOHN
                  (taken aback)
          Okay, okay, I'll plead guilty.

                    PUBLIC DEFENDER
          You'll plead guilty and apologize.

                    JOHN
          I'll plead guilty and apologize.

     The public defender checks his/her watch again.

                    JOHN (CONT'D)
          You still haven't told me your
          name...

                    PUBLIC DEFENDER
                  (impatiently)
          Hush up, it's almost time.

     The public defender looks up at the TV, which is still
     staticky. John looks up at the TV, which is still staticky.

                    JOHN
          What time is it anyway?

                    PUBLIC DEFENDER
          Shush...

The public defender looks up at the TV, which is still
staticky. John looks up at the TV, which is still staticky.

                    JOHN
          Excuse me, but...

The static goes away from the TV screen and a judge appears
on screen.

                    TV JUDGE
               (looking down at a paper)
          Let's move on to the next case...
          The City versus John Doe... John
          Doe?

                    PUBLIC DEFENDER
               (standing up)
          Yes, your honor, we're here.

                    TV JUDGE
          I see that... What's this John Doe
          nonsense?

                    PUBLIC DEFENDER
          Yes, sir. The defendant is
          experiencing memory issues as the
          result of a head injury.

                    TV JUDGE
               (smirking)
          Is that right?

                    PUBLIC DEFENDER
          Yes, your honor.

                    TV JUDGE
          I was directing the question to
          the defendant.

John struggles to stand up.

                    JOHN
               (mumbles)
          Yes, your honor.

                    TV JUDGE
What? I can't hear you. Speak up!

                    JOHN
              (struggling)
I said, yes, your honor.

                    TV JUDGE
My god, man, what happened to your
face?

                    JOHN
I got beat up, your honor.

                    TV JUDGE
While in custody, I suppose.

                    JOHN
Yes, your honor, when I was in the
cell.

                    TV JUDGE
And I suppose your head injury and
loss of memory is being blamed on
the arresting officer.

                    JOHN
No, sir, I didn't say that.

                    PUBLIC DEFENDER
If I may interject, your honor. At
no time did the defendant suggest
to me that he was the victim of
police brutality.

                    TV JUDGE
Fine... So the defendant is on the
record that he does not hold the
city responsible for injuries
sustained while he was custody?

                    PUBLIC DEFENDER
Correct, your honor.

                    TV JUDGE
I want to hear it from him!

                    JOHN
              (mumbling again)
I do not hold the city
responsible...

                    TV JUDGE
Speak up!

                    JOHN
            (louder, as blood starts
            dripping from his mouth)
        I do not hold the city responsible
        for any injuries I received while
        in custody, your honor.

                TV JUDGE
        Including the arresting officer?

                    JOHN
        Yes, sir, including the arresting
        officer.

                TV JUDGE
            (looking down at a paper)
        Now, these charges against you...
        Aggressive Panhandling and
        Assault... Can the defendant
        explain to me how he came to be
        charged?

John glances over to the public defender, who ignores him.

                    JOHN
        I plead guilty, your honor.

                TV JUDGE
        Did I ask you how you plead?

                    JOHN
        Your honor?

                TV JUDGE
        Counsel, did I ask the defendant
        how he pleads?

                PUBLIC DEFENDER
        No, your honor.

                TV JUDGE
        No, I did not. I simply asked the
        defendant how he came to be
        arrested.

                    JOHN
        I apologize, your honor.

                TV JUDGE
        Very well then.

                    JOHN
        And the answer is... I don't
        remember.

                    TV JUDGE
          You don't remember?

                    JOHN
          Correct, sir.

                    TV JUDGE
          But you're ready to plead guilty?

                    JOHN
          Yes, your honor.

                    TV JUDGE
          That doesn't make any sense...
          Does that make sense to you,
          Counselor?

                    PUBLIC DEFENDER
          Well, the defendant has the utmost
          respect for the arresting officer,
          so he is willing to accept the
          charges as witnessed by the
          officer.

                    TV JUDGE
          Bullcrap! I think I now know
          what's going on here with these
          memory loss shenanigans.

                    PUBLIC DEFENDER
          Your honor?

                    TV JUDGE
          Yes, the defendant is homeless and
          was out panhandling, when he saw a
          police officer and thought he
          might get himself arrested. Now he
          wants to become a ward of the
          state and obtain free mental
          health care because of his
          so-called amnesia.

                    JOHN
               (surprised)
          Wait! That's not it at all... I
          mean, I would appreciate some
          help, but I'm not trying to become
          a ward of anyone.

                    TV JUDGE
          Well, you'll get no help from me.
          I'm prepared to accept your plea
          and sentence you to the one night
          you already spent in custody.

                    JOHN
          But your honor...

                    TV JUDGE
                  (interrupting)
          But nothing! Maybe you should
          consider cleaning yourself up,
          finding a job and supporting
          yourself!

The TV suddenly switches back to being staticky and consumes
the entire screen of the camera, creating a segue into the
next scene.

SCENE 06 - EXT. DAY. PARK

John is seen walking in a city park. He approaches a large
fountain. Two teenagers are seen watching him and laughing.
John sits down on the edge of the fountain and leans down
toward the water. He can see his reflection in the water and
is shocked by his appearance.

> JOHN
> (mumbling to himself)
> I don't recognize you, but you
> sure are messed up... No wonder
> the judge told me to clean myself
> up.

John reaches down with both hands to scoop up some water and
splash it onto his face. He reaches down again to repeat the
process, but doesn't notice the teens approaching him from
behind. As John splashes more water onto his face, the teens
suddenly push John into the fountain.

> FOUNTAIN TEEN ONE
> (yells)
> You need to wash more than your
> face, you dirty bum!

As John splashes around in the fountain, trying to stand up,
the teens all laugh at his dilemma and then run away. John
eventually climbs out of the fountain, soaking wet. He then
finds his way to an empty park bench and sits down. There is
a trash can next to the bench. John watches people as they
walk by and ignore him. A young couple then walks toward
John. The man is carrying a fast food bag.

> PARK MAN
> (looks down toward John)
> Hey, Swampy, you hungry? We got
> some food left.

> JOHN
> (looks up)
> I'd be much obliged, thank you...

The man walks past John and tosses the food bag into the
trash can.

> PARK MAN
> (laughing)
> Then you can work and dig it out
> of the trash, lazy bum!

The woman laughs along with the man as they walk away. John
slides across the bench and retrieves the food bag. He
inspects the contents and it looks disgusting. John still
eats the leftover food from the bag.

SCENE 07 - EXT. DAY. PUBLIC ASSISTANCE BUILDING

A series of shots show John aimlessly walking the streets of
the city as though he was invisible to all the inhabitants.
He eventually passes a large building with signage
indicating PUBLIC ASSISTANCE. He enters the building.

SCENE 08 - INT. DAY. PUBLIC ASSISTANCE BUILDING

John peeks into a nondescript office and sees a social
worker behind the desk.

                    JOHN
          Excuse me, are you still open?

                    SOCIAL WORKER
                    (checking watch)
          Not for long, we close at five...
          How can I help you?

John enters the office and takes a seat in front of the
desk.

                    JOHN
          I am seeking assistance.

                    SOCIAL WORKER
          With what?

                    JOHN
          Well, just look at me. I mean
          isn't it obvious I need help?

                    SOCIAL WORKER
          Sir, lots of people drop by their
          local thrift shop, buy some rags,
          dirty themselves up, and try to
          scam the government.

                    JOHN
          Oh, well that's not me. I am
          legitimately in need of
          assistance.

                    SOCIAL WORKER
          You'll have to be more specific.

                    JOHN
          I'm homeless, for one. And I'm
          also hungry.

                    SOCIAL WORKER
          I didn't hear anything about
          wanting a job.

                    JOHN
          Don't get me wrong, I'm not afraid
          to work...

                    SOCIAL WORKER
                (begins typing on desktop
                computer)
            Okay, then, let's start with your
            name.

                    JOHN
            I don... I don't know.

                    SOCIAL WORKER
            First name, Ida? Spelled I-D-A?

                    JOHN
            No, I'm not sure what my name is.

                    SOCIAL WORKER
                (looking away from computer
                screen to face John)
            So you want public assistance
            without identifying yourself?

                    JOHN
            Please understand that I'm not
            trying to deceive anyone. I really
            cannot remember what my name is or
            anything else from my past.

                    SOCIAL WORKER
            Seriously?

                    JOHN
            Seriously, I was recently injured,
            or attacked, and I woke up
            underneath a bridge with amnesia.

                    SOCIAL WORKER
            So you've been wandering around
            town with a serious head injury?

                    JOHN
            Yes! And hoping somebody will help
            me!

Social worker checks his/her wristwatch, shuts down the
computer and stands up from the desk. John watches the
social worker's activities, waiting for a response.

                    JOHN (CONT'D)
            So, can you help me?

                    SOCIAL WORKER
                (starting to walk past John)
            I'm afraid it's five o'clock.
            Thank you for stopping by.

The social worker reaches the office doorway and reaches up
to touch the light switch. John stands up to face the social
worker, but doesn't approach.

>   SOCIAL WORKER (CONT'D)
>   The office is closed for the day.
>   You'll have to leave now, Mister
>   Whoever-You-Are.

>   JOHN
>   (getting angry)
>   No! I won't leave here until I get
>   some help! I need help! Can't you
>   see that?

The social worker walks back toward John.

>   SOCIAL WORKER
>   Sure, I know you could use some
>   help, but the assistance you need
>   immediately appears to be medical.
>   The nearest emergency room is five
>   blocks away.

>   JOHN
>   Oh...

>   SOCIAL WORKER
>   But I pass it on my way home, so
>   if you want me to drive you there,
>   I would be glad to assist.

SCENE 09 - INT. NIGHT. HOSPITAL EMERGENCY ROOM

John is seated by himself in a waiting area, away from other patients in a hospital emergency room. A wall clock is positioned above his seat. The social worker approaches and sits down next to John.

                    SOCIAL WORKER
          Listen, I've explained your
          situation to the nurse in charge.
          She's going to have a doctor take
          a look at your injuries. She knows
          you cannot provide your name and
          that you have no ability to pay.
          She has opened a case file for you
          under John Doe.

                    JOHN
          Thank you.

                    SOCIAL WORKER
                  (standing up)
          Well, you'll have to be patient,
          no pun intended. The nurse says
          they'll get to you when they can.

As the social worker exits the emergency room, the camera focuses on a wall clock above where John is seated... The clock then shows two hours have passed.

SCENE 10 - INT. NIGHT. HOSPITAL EXAMINATION ROOM

John is sitting on an examination table as a doctor
examines him. The doctor is checking his pulse, heartbeat
and looking into his ears and pupils.

> HOSPITAL DOCTOR
> You say your jaw hurts too?

> JOHN
> Yes, doctor.

> HOSPITAL DOCTOR
> (placing his gloved hand
> under John's chin)
> Open your mouth as wide as you
> can.

> JOHN
> Ahhhh...

> HOSPITAL DOCTOR
> (moving John's lower jaw
> around and observing)
> "Ahhhh" isn't necessary.

> JOHN
> (once the doctor lets go of
> his chin)
> Sorry, doc.

> HOSPITAL DOCTOR
> Any loose teeth?

> JOHN
> I don't think so...

> HOSPITAL DOCTOR
> Okay, lean your head towards me,
> Mister Doe.

The doctor begins looking around John's head until he finds
the injury.

> HOSPITAL DOCTOR (CONT'D)
> Yes, sir, that's one nasty bump
> you've got there. I assume you're
> still feeling some pain from it.

> JOHN
> (still with his head down)
> Yes, doctor. Sometimes it's bad
> and sometimes not so bad, but the
> pain is always there.

> HOSPITAL DOCTOR
> Okay, you can sit back up... Are
> you feeling any dizziness?

> JOHN
> The dizziness comes in spells.
> When I start to feel dizzy, I
> usually have to sit down for a
> while.

> HOSPITAL DOCTOR
> Blurry vision?

> JOHN
> Yes, but I don't even remember if
> I wore glasses. So maybe the
> blurriness is not from the injury.

> HOSPITAL DOCTOR
> How about indigestion, sick to the
> stomach?

> JOHN
> Well, to be honest, doctor, I
> haven't had much to eat to cause
> any indigestion.

> HOSPITAL DOCTOR
> But you have an appetite?

> JOHN
> Oh, yeah, you know it!

The doctor takes a step back and observes John, as if
contemplating what to do; he then types some information
into a computer on a stand.

> HOSPITAL DOCTOR
> (still looking at the
> computer screen and typing)
> Okay, Mister Doe, you've obviously
> experienced a concussion. I am
> going to order a CT Scan for you,
> in order to determine the extent
> of any damage to your skull and
> brain.

> JOHN
> And my jaw?

> HOSPITAL DOCTOR
> Yes, we'll check that too.

                    JOHN
Will I be spending the night at
the hospital?

                HOSPITAL DOCTOR
             (looks at John and chuckles)

I don't think so. Not unless we
find excessive pressure or
bleeding.

                    JOHN
                (disappointed)
Oh.

                HOSPITAL DOCTOR
After your CT Scan, you'll return
to the waiting room. I will come
out to tell you the results as
soon as I review the x-rays.

                    JOHN
Okay. Thank you.

SCENE 11 - INT. NIGHT. HOSPITAL EMERGENCY ROOM

John is once again sitting in the waiting area of the
emergency room, in his original seat with the wall clock
above him. The clock shows another couple hours have passed.

The hospital doctor approaches with a clipboard and sits
down next to John. John appears to be sleeping.

                    HOSPITAL DOCTOR
                 (nudges John)
            Are you awake, Mister Doe?

John stirs and is awakened.

                    JOHN
            Wha-what?

                    HOSPITAL DOCTOR
                 (relieved)
            Oh, thank god. I thought you were
            dead.

                    JOHN
            Dead?

                    HOSPITAL DOCTOR
                 (looks down at
                 the clipboard)
            Well, Mister Doe, I have looked at
            the results of the CT scan and
            determined that you did indeed
            experience a concussion and your
            skull has a slight fracture, which
            should heal on its own. There's no
            apparent brain damage. I wouldn't
            even recommend stitches for the
            small cut...

                    JOHN
            But what about the amnesia?

                    HOSPITAL DOCTOR
            Oh, yes, the amnesia... Well, I'm
            no brain surgeon or psychiatrist,
            but what you likely have is called
            post-traumatic amnesia. I believe
            you'll eventually begin to regain
            your memory, but it may take
            weeks, or even months, to fully
            recover.

                    JOHN
            (shaking his head in dismay)
    Weeks or even months to remember
    who I am?

                    HOSPITAL DOCTOR
            (hands John pill bottle)
    Possibly... In the meantime, I
    have some ibuprofen here to help
    with the pain. I also suggest you
    have social services help you find
    a homeless shelter. You'll recover
    faster if you're out of the
    elements.

                    JOHN
    This is... This whole ordeal is
    just so depressing... You can't
    imagine, doc.

                    HOSPITAL DOCTOR
    Well, I do have some good news.

                    JOHN
    What's that?

                    HOSPITAL DOCTOR
    Your jaw looks okay.

SCENE 12 - EXT. NIGHT. HOSPITAL EMERGENCY ROOM

It is dark and John is seen exiting the hospital emergency
room. He walks down to the sidewalk and begins walking in
the direction of midtown, where some tall lighted buildings
are visible.

                    JOHN
                 (mumbling to himself)
            Maybe I'll make it to the Public
            Assistance office when it opens...

SCENE 13 - EXT. NIGHT. CITY STREETS

In a series of shots, John is seen walking on various
sidewalks as he heads to the center of the city. He
eventually comes upon a stand-alone pizza shop.

SCENE 14 - EXT. NIGHT. PIZZA SHOP

John slowly approaches the pizza shop, where he observes
employees leaving the store, saying their goodbyes and
driving off. One last employee turns off the lights of the
shop and locks the front door. This employee also gets in a
nearby vehicle and drives off site.

John waits until he is sure no one else is around, then he
walks around the side of the building where he finds a large
garbage dumpster. John struggles to open the heavy lid. He
looks inside, and then tries to reach down inside, but he
comes up with nothing. He looks around to make sure no one
is watching and then begins to climb inside. He ends up
falling inside. In the dim light of the parking lot, he
finds a discarded pizza and begins eating.

Another shot of the parking lot shows a vagrant couple
creeping up toward the dumpster. The female is walking with
a cane, while the male is carrying a flashlight.

                    FEMALE VAGRANT
          The lid is up!

                    MALE VAGRANT
          Hush your mouth.

The male vagrant turns on his flashlight as he comes up on
the open dumpster. As the female comes up to the side of the
dumpster, the male shines the flashlight beam into the
dumpster. The beam illuminates John with a slice of pizza
hanging from his mouth.

John shields his eyes from the bright glare of the
flashlight.

                    JOHN
               (garbled from the food)
          What's going on?

                    MALE VAGRANT
          What do you think you're doing in
          there?!

                    JOHN
               (spits out some pizza)
          I'm eating pizza.

                    FEMALE VAGRANT
          Our pizza, you mean!

                    JOHN
          I think there's plenty here... We
          can share.

                    MALE VAGRANT
               (raising the flashlight as
               if to strike down on John)
          No, we ain't sharin' our pizza!
          This is our dumpster! Ever'body
          knows that!

                    JOHN
               (raising his arms to protect
               himself)
          Please, I didn't know! I'm new to
          town! I'll leave the dumpster
          right now and won't ever come
          back!

The female vagrant walks around the back of the dumpster.
The male vagrant suddenly backs away from the dumpster. The
female then slams the lid shut.

                    MALE VAGRANT
               (shouts)
          Here girl! Bring me that cane!

The female vagrant comes back to the front of the dumpster
and hands the cane to the male. The male vagrant slips the
cane through a slot on the lid, securing it so it cannot be
opened from the inside. John's muffled voice can be heard
from within the dumpster and he can also be heard banging
the sides and lid.

                    MALE VAGRANT (CONT'D)
          There! That should hold him! I'll
          gitcha a new cane, girl, but that
          fella needed taught a lesson!

The vagrant couple leave the property. The female is limping
a bit from the loss of her cane.

SCENE 15 - EXT. DAWN. PIZZA SHOP

As dawn breaks, a garbage truck is seen backing up to the pizza shop's dumpster. The back end of the truck bumps into dumpster, causing a loud crashing sound. Some kind of hitch device lowers from the truck and attaches to the top of the dumpster. The dumpster is then lifted into the air, turned upside down and shaken over top of the truck. But nothing empties from the dumpster because the lid is locked shut.

> SANITARY ENGINEER ONE
> (looks over at the driver)
> I don't think it emptied.

> SANITARY ENGINEER TWO
> (at the wheel)
> I didn't hear nuthin either.

> SANITARY ENGINEER ONE
> (opening the truck door)
> Lower 'er down and I'll take a
> look.

After the dumpster is slammed back onto the ground, sanitary engineer one approaches it.

> SANITARY ENGINEER ONE (CONT'D)
> (yells to the driver)
> I think I see the problem!
> Somebody jammed a stick into the
> lid!

Sanitary engineer one loosens the cane and pulls it off. He tosses the cane aside and makes sure the lid will open.

> JOHN
> (barely audible)
> Help me...

> SANITARY ENGINEER ONE
> What the heck was that?

Sanitary engineer one opens the lid wider and sees John covered in garbage.

> SANITARY ENGINEER ONE (CONT'D)
> (angry)
> What are you doin' in there?!

> JOHN
> (barely audible)
> Help me...

Sanitary engineer one reaches down and grabs John's arm, pulling up John violently to his feet.

                    SANITARY ENGINEER ONE
              Git outta there right now!

                         JOHN
                      (pleading)
              But I think I'm hurt...

                    SANITARY ENGINEER ONE
                 (angrily grabbing John)
              I tole you to git out the
              dumpster!

Sanitary engineer one grabs John with both hands and forces
him over the side of the dumpster and onto ground. John
screams in pain as he hits the cement.

                    SANITARY ENGINEER ONE (CONT'D)
              Now git!

John half limps, half crawls away.

                    SANITARY ENGINEER ONE (CONT'D)
                 (yells to the driver)
              Okay, bud, let's try this agin!

SCENE 16 - EXT. MORNING. CITY STREETS

Shots of John limping along various sidewalks. His clothes
are shredded and covered in stains from the dumpster. His
face is distraught with anguish and he is mumbling to
himself.

> JOHN
> (mumbling softly)
> Why me... Why me...

John eventually approaches a public drinking fountain. He
reaches inside his jacket for his ibuprofen, but doesn't
find it right away. He begins desperately patting down his
jacket and tearing through his empty pockets.

> JOHN (CONT'D)
> (in desperation)
> My pills! Where are my pills! My
> pills!... I've lost them! I've
> lost my pills!

John collapses onto the ground and begins sobbing.
Pedestrians walk around him/over him.

SCENE 17 - EXT. MORNING. BRIDGE

John is now straddling the railing of a high bridge, one leg
over the edge and one leg still on the sidewalk. He seems in
a daze and his face is twitching.

                    JOHN
               (whispers to himself)
          I've got to end this now... I
          don't know what or who I was
          before, but I darn well know what
          I've just gone through... I'm in
          constant pain and misery with no
          one willing to help me. There's
          only one way that I can finally
          end this pain... Forget whatever
          happened in the past... I don't
          even care anymore.

John tries to lift his stationary leg from the surface of
the sidewalk, but realizes he cannot. He tries a second time
to lift the leg and hears growling.

                    JOHN (CONT'D)
               (looking down at the
                sidewalk side)
          What's going on?

John looks down and sees a dog tugging at his pant leg.

                    JOHN (CONT'D)
          Hey! Let go! Get out of here! What
          are doing, mutt?

John tries to shake the dog from his pant leg, but the dog
refuses to let go and continues to growl.

                    JOHN (CONT'D)
          If you make me get up, I swear
          I'll kick your mangy butt! Go
          away!

The dog refuses to let go and continues to growl. John
twists his other leg back over the railing and he ends up
falling down onto the sidewalk.

The dog lets go of the pant leg and attempts to lick John's
face. John pushes the dog away. The dog then lays down
beside John on the sidewalk.

John looks down at the dog beside him and shakes his head.

                    JOHN (CONT'D)
              What's wrong with you, boy? Do I
              have to go find a different
              bridge?

John uses the railing as leverage in order to slowly get to
his feet. The dog then jumps up on its feet. John begins to
hobble off, leaving the dog behind.

The dog barks at John. John doesn't acknowledge. The dog
barks again at John. John turns around.

The dog begins walking in the opposite direction.

                    JOHN (CONT'D)
                 (yelling toward the dog)
              Seriously, you want me to go that
              direction?

The dog turns around to face John and barks.

                    JOHN (CONT'D)
                 (still yelling)
              Okay, okay, already! But slow
              down, I don't walk so well!

Camera moves into a close-up of John as he limps along. His
face does not seem so distraught anymore.

                    JOHN (CONT'D)
                 (mumbling to himself)
              What do I care which direction I
              walk...

SCENE 18 - EXT. DAY. CITY SIDEWALKS

Shots of John and the dog walking on various city sidewalks.
The dog eventually leads John to the City Mission and stops.

SCENE 19 - EXT. DAY. CITY MISSION

The dog stops in front of the door of the City Mission.

                    JOHN
          The City Mission, eh?

The dog barks in response.

                    JOHN (CONT'D)
          You want me to go in there?

The dog barks in response.

John begins to walk into the Mission. Once he is through the
threshold, he turns around to look at the dog.

                    JOHN (CONT'D)
          You coming in too?

The dog barks in response.

John begins to walk back out, but then notices a sign taped
to some glass near the doorway. The sign says NO PETS
ALLOWED.

                    JOHN (CONT'D)
                 (points to the sign)
          Oh, I see... But you'll wait for
          me, right?

The dog barks in response. John re-enters the Mission.

SCENE 20 - INT. DAY. MISSION.

John limps into the Mission and looks around. A Pastor meets
him near the door.

> PASTOR
> Welcome, brother. You look
> injured. Please come in and have a
> seat.

> JOHN
> Thank you, Father.

> PASTOR
> Of course, of course. Please sit
> at this table.

John sits at a small table and the Pastor sits opposite him.

> PASTOR (CONT'D)
> And what has brought you here
> today, sir?

> JOHN
> A dog.

> PASTOR
> Excuse me?

> JOHN
> A dog brought me here, straight to
> your door. I was about to hurl
> myself from a bridge and this dog
> suddenly pulls me off the railing.

> PASTOR
> That's astonishing. So a dog saved
> your life?

> JOHN
> A dog saved me from taking my
> life, but I really have no life to
> speak of... Certainly no life
> worth saving.

> PASTOR
> That's nonsense. God didn't give
> you life for you to just end it on
> your own.

                    JOHN
          Then why did God allow me to be
          injured so severely that I can no
          longer remember my name or who I
          used to be?

                    PASTOR
          Well, I know at this time you
          certainly don't want to hear me
          preaching about God working in
          mysterious ways...

                    JOHN
               (small laugh)
          You got that right, Father.

                    PASTOR
          Fair enough. Would you like me to
          get you some food?

                    JOHN
          Yes, Father, I am so hungry...

                    PASTOR
               (standing up)
          I'll be right back.

As the Pastor leaves the table, John looks around the room.
He sees some other homeless people milling about, but they
all avert their eyes when John looks at them. To show the
short passage of time, there are brief shots of other
homeless folks keeping themselves busy, like reading or
playing cards at other tables.

Soon the Pastor returns with a tray of food and places it in
front of John.

                    PASTOR (CONT'D)
          Hopefully, this will be to your
          liking.

                    JOHN
               (looking down at the tray)
          I'm sure it will be, Father. Thank
          you again.

                    PASTOR
               (walks behind John's chair
               and places his hand on
               John's shoulders)
          Before you begin, let's take a
          moment to thank God for this food.

John lowers his head and clasps his hand in prayer.

>   PASTOR (CONT'D)
>   Lord God, Heavenly Father, bless
>   us and these Thy gifts which we
>   receive from Thy bountiful
>   goodness, through Jesus Christ,
>   our Lord. Amen.

>   JOHN
>   Amen.

>   PASTOR
>   (walking around the table to
>   face John)
>   Take your time brother... I will
>   be nearby, but I now have to look
>   after the needs of others.

>   JOHN
>   I'm not going anywhere, Father.

>   PASTOR
>   That's very good, because I'd like
>   to talk to you more once you've
>   finished your meal.

>   JOHN
>   Okay.

The Pastor walks away and John begins to eat. John has what
appears to be a bowl of stew with hunks of meat in it. John
takes a napkin from the tray and places it on his lap. As he
eats, he occasionally looks up at the others in the room to
determine if anyone is watching him. If no one is looking at
him, he quickly drops a piece of meat onto his lap. He
continues this activity of eating and dropping meat until
the stew is gone. He eventually takes a drink of whatever
beverage is in front of him, rolls the napkin into a ball,
and stands up from the table. He then slinks out of the
Mission door.

SCENE 21 - EXT. DAY. CITY MISSION

John exits the Mission and see the dog sitting on the
sidewalk. John kneels beside the dog, opens the napkin, and
places the food in front of the dog.

                    JOHN
          Here boy, look what I brought for
          you.

The dog excitedly wags its tail and begins to eat the meat.
As John watches the dog eat, he tears up.

                    JOHN (CONT'D)
                (crying)
          Thank you, boy. Thank you for
          saving my life... You've given me
          hope. Thank you so much.

When the dog finishes eating the meat, John reaches over and
hugs the dog. The dog licks his face.

SCENE 22 - INT. DAY. MISSION.

John re-enters the Mission to find the Pastor praying at the table where he was previously seated. The tray is missing. As John approaches the table, the Pastor looks up.

> PASTOR
>> Oh, thank God, you've returned...
>> I thought you might have left us
>> for good.

> JOHN
>> (sitting down opposite the
>> Pastor)
>> Of course not. You said you wanted
>> to continue our conversation.

> PASTOR
>> Indeed I do... In fact, this is
>> the time when I usually ask our
>> new guests what their name is. But
>> I know you can't tell me that.

> JOHN
>> Not at this time... A doctor last
>> night told me it could be weeks or
>> months before I regain my memory.

> PASTOR
>> So presently, you have no
>> recollection of events prior to
>> your injury?

> JOHN
>> Correct, Father.

> PASTOR
>> That raises an interesting
>> theological question that I must
>> ask.

> JOHN
>> Okay...

> PASTOR
>> (leans in closer to John)
>> Do you know if you've been Saved?

                    JOHN
You mean Saved by the Lord?

                    PASTOR
Yes! Born again!

                    JOHN
I said I had no memory prior to my
injury.

                    PASTOR
I know, I know. But this is
different. If you've been Born
Again, Jesus entered your heart
and soul, and He should still be
there.

                    JOHN
I know what you want me to say, of
course, to validate your beliefs,
but I'm just not sure...

                    PASTOR
I remember the day I asked Christ
to enter my heart, but even if I
didn't remember I think I would
still know that He was there. He's
there, guiding everything I say
and everything I do.

                    JOHN
He may be with me also Father,
guiding me, but He doesn't make
His presence known.

                    PASTOR
Do you pray?

                    JOHN
Not lately, Father. But I may have
in the past.

                    PASTOR
Even with your loss of memory, I'd
like to think you would have tried
prayer during your recent
tribulations, especially if you
had previously been introduced to
Christ.

                    JOHN
         I'd like to think I was Born
         Again, but maybe I haven't. I
         mean, just look at my tattoos

                    PASTOR
         Looks can be deceiving, my
         brother. For instance, my heart
         tells me you're a thoughtful,
         gentle man who cares about
         others... A head injury doesn't
         bring about sudden empathy.

                    JOHN
         I know that I have no malice
         toward anyone who has mistreated
         me. In fact, I feel sorry for
         folks who can be so cold-hearted
         and mean-spirited.

                    PASTOR
         Your words are reminiscent of
         Christ and spoken like a true
         Christian. That's why I can't help
         but believe you are Born Again.

                    JOHN
         If you say so...

                    PASTOR
         As Christ was dying on the cross,
         He forgave those who tormented
         Him. You have the same attribute
         of forgiveness within you.

                    JOHN
         But are you saying that a person
         cannot be gentle and forgiving
         without having Christ in their
         heart?

                    PASTOR
         Of course not. I know there are
         many agnostics whose nature it is
         to treat others with love and
         kindness. I just think your
         compassion is more in line with
         Christian faith.

                    JOHN
         Like I said, I'd like to think
         I've been Born Again.

                    PASTOR
              (reaching across the table
              to grasp John's hands)
         Look inside yourself, my son. Pray
         with me...

                    JOHN
              (lowering his head in
              prayer)
         Sure, Father.

                    PASTOR
              (praying)
         Heavenly Father, if this good man
         has accepted You into his heart,
         please make your presence known to
         him. For once he is certain he has
         been Saved, perhaps other fond
         memories will come back to him and
         flood his soul with joy. Just as
         Christ rose again from the crypt
         to live again, we pray that our
         friend rises out of his state of
         amnesia to live the life that he
         once lived. Amen.

                    JOHN
         Amen.

The two men raise their heads and look at each other across
the table.

                    PASTOR
         I assume you would like a bed for
         the night.

                    JOHN
         I would be most appreciative.

                    PASTOR
         I'll also take you down to the
         clothes donation room to see if
         anything fits you.

                    JOHN
         Thank you.

                    PASTOR
         And in the morning, I would hope
         you'd join us in the chapel for a
         sermon.

                    JOHN
         I certainly will, Father.

SCENE 23 - INT. NIGHT. MISSION DORMITORY

The camera begins with a wide shot of various people at the
Mission preparing to go to bed on their individual cots. The
camera closes in on John kneeling in prayer in front of his
cot. He is wearing different clothes. The camera catches
items on his cot, including a pocket-sized Bible, a new bag
of underwear and a new bag of socks. John is praying, but
not aloud.

SCENE 24 - INT. DAY. MISSION CHAPEL

The camera shows a small one-room chapel with single
cheap-looking chairs representing pews. The chairs are
sparsely filled with a few people. John is shown sitting in
the back row.

Eventually the Pastor enters the chapel and takes his place
behind a podium.

                    PASTOR
          I'm sorry we have no hymnals or
          musical accompaniment, but if you
          know this hymn, I hope you'll sing
          along with me...

                    PASTOR (CONT'D)
                    (a Capella)
          Amazing grace, How sweet the sound

          That saved a wretch like me.

          I once was lost, but now I am
          found,

          Was blind, but now I see.

At first it seems only the Pastor is singing. The camera
shows disinterested faces of some of the patrons. Finally
the camera shows a close-up of John, who seems anxious to
remember the lyrics.

                    PASTOR (CONT'D)
          'Twas grace that taught my heart
          to fear,

          And grace my fears relieved.

          How precious did that grace appear

          The hour I first believed.

After returning to the Pastor, the camera switches again to
John, who actually sings the words "I have already come."

>   PASTOR (CONT'D)
> Through many dangers, toils and
> snares
>
> I have already come,
>
> 'Tis grace has brought me safe
> thus far
>
> And grace will lead me home.

Back to the Pastor, then the camera shows John sing "He will my shield and portion be, as long as life endures"

>   PASTOR (CONT'D)
> The Lord has promised good to me
>
> His word my hope secures;
>
> He will my shield and portion be,
>
> As long as life endures.

The Pastor notices John trying to remember the lyrics and walks to the back of the chapel where John is standing.

>   PASTOR (CONT'D)
> Yea, when this flesh and heart
> shall fail,
>
> And mortal life shall cease
>
> I shall possess within the veil,
>
> A life of joy and peace.

The Pastor and John are now standing together and singing the final refrain:

>   PASTOR AND JOHN
>   (singing joyfully)
> When we've been there ten thousand
> years
>
> Bright shining as the sun,
>
> We've no less days to sing God's
> praise
>
> Than when we've first begun.

The two men finish the song and embrace. John then sits down and the Pastor returns to the podium/pulpit. The camera remains on the Pastor as he delivers the sermon.

PASTOR
(opening a book at the
podium/pulpit)

One of the miracles that God gives
us every day is the birth of a
child. Whether it be the birth of
a son or daughter, or a grandchild
- or our own birth.

Of course, no one asked us if we
wanted to be born, or to whom we
wanted born. From the moment we
left the womb, we were suddenly
thrust into an environment where
we needed to learn to survive.

We may have been born into a poor
family or an abusive family and
wondered why God would place us
there, instead of in a grand
mansion surrounded by nannies who
would feed us the best baby food
from silver spoons and fine china.

But the greatest of God's miracles
is not our physical birth, but our
Spiritual birth.

Yes, I say that the Spiritual
birth of a lost sinner into
spiritual life is the most
miraculous gift that God offers
mankind!

PASTOR (CONT'D)
Why is Spiritual birth more
miraculous than physical birth?
Because when we are Born Again,
God allows us to escape the pains
of Death in this life and grants
us Eternal Life in Heaven.

When I was a student in seminary,
my instructor, Father Daniels,
asked the class to describe the
essence of being Born Again. We
students all knew that we were
Born Again and had Christ in our
hearts, but we had great
difficulty in putting the
experience into words.

PASTOR (CONT'D)
I still have my notes from that
day and this is how Father Daniels
explained the Spiritual state of
being Born Again:

"To be born again doesn't mean
that a good person just becomes a
really good person...

"Or that a moral person just
becomes an even more moral person;

"Or that a church member simply
becomes an even better church
member.

"To be Born Again means that a
spiritually bankrupt person gains
all of the promises and blessings
that God promises to those who are
His. It means that a totally
depraved, wicked person is
completely cleansed of all his or
her sins. It means that a person
who has absolutely nothing to
offer to God is freely given the
greatest gift that they could
possibly receive, and that is
Eternal Life. It means that
someone who is completely and
totally rotten to the core becomes
a child of God. Who is that
spiritually bankrupt person, that
totally depraved wicked person,
that person who has absolutely
nothing to offer to God, that
person who is completely and
totally rotten to the core? That
person is you. That person is me."

Now I would like to read from
John, Chapter Three, Verses one
through eight:

Now there was a Pharisee, a man
named Nicodemus, who was a member
of the Jewish ruling council. He
came to Jesus at night and said,
"Rabbi, we know that you are a
teacher who has come from God. For
no one could perform the signs you
are doing if God were not with
him."

> PASTOR (CONT'D)
> Jesus replied, "Very truly I tell
> you, no one can see the kingdom of
> God unless they are Born Again."

> "How can someone be born when they
> are old?" Nicodemus asked. "Surely
> they cannot enter a second time
> into their mother's womb to be
> born!"

> Jesus answered, "Very truly I tell
> you, no one can enter the kingdom
> of God unless they are born of
> water and the Spirit. Flesh gives
> birth to flesh, but the Spirit[b]
> gives birth to spirit. You should
> not be surprised at my saying,
> 'You must be Born Again.' The wind
> blows wherever it pleases. You
> hear its sound, but you cannot
> tell where it comes from or where
> it is going. So it is with
> everyone born of the Spirit."

> PASTOR (CONT'D)
> (looks up from the
> podium/pulpit)
> Tell me, brothers... Is there
> anyone here this morning who wants
> to hear the sanctifying sound of
> God's breath blowing through your
> soul?

All the people in the audience stand. Everyone but John
leave the chapel. John walks boldly to the front of the
chapel near the podium/pulpit. John is at the front row of
empty seats when he kneels in front of the podium/pulpit.
The Pastor leaves his place at the podium/pulpit and
approaches John, who is still kneeling with his head down.
The Pastor sits down in an empty chair beside John.

> PASTOR (CONT'D)
> Have you decided to be Saved,
> brother?

> JOHN
> (voice breaking)
> Last night I had the most horrific
> nightmares, Father. They were so
> vivid and so real to me. I was a
> young man in the dreams and I did
> terrible things.

                    PASTOR
              (placing his hand on John's
              trembling shoulder)
          They may only have been dreams, my
          son, with no basis in reality or
          your past... Everyone has bad
          dreams every once in a while.

                    JOHN
          But I can't take the chance that I
          possibly could have done any of
          the sinful things I saw in my
          dreams... I feel like, if I had
          sinned that way as a young man,
          then Christ would have forgiven me
          upon my being Saved - and I would
          no longer be troubled by such
          nightmares.

                    PASTOR
              (leaning down closer to
              John)
          Very well... He was in the world,
          and the world was made through
          Him, and the world did not know
          Him. He came to His own, and those
          who were His own did not receive
          Him. But as many as received Him,
          to them He gave the right to
          become children of God, even to
          those who believe in His name, who
          were born, not of blood nor of the
          will of the flesh nor of the will
          of man, but of God.

                    JOHN
              (praying)
          Dear Lord Jesus, I know that I am
          a sinner, and I ask for Your
          forgiveness. I believe You died
          for my sins and rose from the
          dead. I turn from my sins and
          invite You to come into my heart
          and life. I want to trust and
          follow You as my Lord and Savior.

     There is a long pause and it is obvious that the Pastor is
     in silently praying.

                    PASTOR
          Where did you learn that, my son?

                    JOHN
          I saw it on a pamphlet last night
          and memorized it. Did I say it
          right?

                    PASTOR
          You said it fine, but as you were
          reciting what is commonly called
          'The Sinner's Prayer,' God
          enlightened me about something
          that is very important.

                    JOHN
          And what was that, Father, if you
          don't mind me asking.

                    PASTOR
          The prayer is fine, even though it
          is not in the Bible. But please
          realize that inviting Christ into
          your heart is just the beginning.
          You must continue to have faith
          and to act accordingly... A man
          can only be saved through faith.
          And faith is much more than
          repeating a formulaic prayer.
          Salvation is achieved through acts
          of faith.

                    JOHN
               (standing up)
          From this point forward, I shall
          walk in faith with my Savior,
          Jesus Christ.

John turns from the Pastor and walks boldly from the chapel.

SCENE 25 - EXT. DAY. CITY MISSION

John exits the Mission, carrying a small plastic bag with
some belongings, and immediately looks up and down the
sidewalk for the dog.

> JOHN
> (calling out)
> Boy, where are you boy?!

He waits for a moment, then looks both ways on the sidewalk
again. The camera comes in close to John's concerned
worrisome face.

> JOHN (CONT'D)
> Boy, come out boy! Please come
> out!

John walks around the corner of the Mission and looks up the
alley.

> JOHN (CONT'D)
> Boy, are you back here?! Where are
> you, boy?!

John solemnly turns around to face the street and begins
walking up the sidewalk.

The camera now shows a very wide shot from across the
street. The wide shot shows John walking back past the
entrance of the Mission until he literally walks out of
frame. The wide shot is now static for a few moments,
showing no one or any activity.

Suddenly the dog runs into frame, past the Mission, and out
of frame in the same direction as John.

SCENE 26 - EXT. DAY. CITY SIDEWALKS

Shots of John and the dog walking on various city sidewalks.

SCENE 27 - EXT. DAY. PARK

John returns to the city park, this time with the dog. They
walk around the perimeter of an empty baseball field. At one
point, John kicks an old raggedy baseball from some weeds.

                    JOHN
              (picking up the ball)
          Hey, boy, you wanna play some
          catch?

Now there is a series of shots of John and the dog playing
fetch in the park. John is still holding his plastic bag of
belongings. One throw goes off target and lands at the feet
of a groundskeeper, who is picking up garbage from the
ground with a "trash picker" rod and depositing the garbage
to a large plastic bag. John and the dog approach the
groundskeeper.

                    JOHN (CONT'D)
          Sorry, sir. I hope I didn't hit
          you.

The groundskeeper leans down to pet the dog and put the
ball in its mouth.

                    GROUNDSKEEPER
              (Looks up at John while
              petting the dog)
          Nah, you didn't hit me... Nice dog
          you got here.

                    JOHN
          Yeah, he kind of adopted me...

The groundskeeper stands back up.

                    JOHN (CONT'D)
          Hey, how do you get a job like
          yours?

                    GROUNDSKEEPER
          You mean picking up trash all day?

                    JOHN
          Yeah, it doesn't look that hard,
          plus you're out in the fresh air
          and getting exercise.

> GROUNDSKEEPER
> (laughs)
> There's no fresh air when you're
> lugging around a heavy bag of
> smelly garbage, putting strain on
> your back and shoulders. Plus,
> the maintenance supervisor only
> pays thirty bucks a day.

> JOHN

Cash?

> GROUNDSKEEPER
> Yes, it's all under the table... I
> think the supervisor guy believes
> he's helping the less fortunate by
> letting people like me do his job,
> while he kicks back in his air-
> conditioned office.

> JOHN
> So, are you thinking
> about quitting?

> GROUNDSKEEPER
> Actually, I have been. In fact, if
> you're interested in the job, I'll
> hand over my rod and bag, and you
> can go check in at the
> supervisor's office near the
> public restrooms over there.

After the groundskeeper points in the direction of the
maintenance office, he hands the trash picker and garbage
bag to John. John is now carrying two plastic bags (a large
trash bag and his smaller bag of belongings).

> GROUNDSKEEPER (CONT'D)
> (smiling)

> At least I found my own
> replacement, instead of leaving
> the supervisor high and dry.

> JOHN
> (accepting the items)
> Thank you. Your rod and bag
> comfort me...

> GROUNDS KEEPER

What?

> JOHN
> Never mind, it was just a bad
> joke.

SCENE 28 - INT. DAY. MAINTENANCE SUPERVISOR'S OFFICE

The park maintenance supervisor is seated behind a desk when
he hears a knock.

                    MAINTENANCE SUPERVISOR
                (calls out)
        Come in.

John comes in carrying the Trash Picker rod.

                    MAINTENANCE SUPERVISOR (CONT'D)
        Don't tell me another one quit?

                    JOHN
        It appears so, but I'm willing to
        be his replacement.

                    MAINTENANCE SUPERVISOR
        Okay, well, come take a seat.

                    JOHN
                (sitting down)
        Thank you, sir.

                    MAINTENANCE SUPERVISOR
        You down on your luck, fella?

                    JOHN
        I guess you could say that... One
        day I woke up under a bridge with
        a head injury.

                    MAINTENANCE SUPERVISOR
        No family or friends to help you?

                    JOHN
        That's the thing. The injury
        caused amnesia and I can't
        remember who my family is, if I
        even have one.

                    MAINTENANCE SUPERVISOR
        Well, I'll help you out, at least
        as far as a job.

                    JOHN
        How about shelter? I noticed the
        attached garage... Can my dog and
        I sleep there until I regain my
        memory and get back on my feet?

                    MAINTENANCE SUPERVISOR
          Hmmm, I suppose so, as long as you
          don't make a mess of the place or
          take anything.

                    JOHN
          No, sir. You won't even know we
          sleep there.

                    MAINTENANCE SUPERVISOR
          Okay, did my ex-employee explain
          to you what the job entails?

                    JOHN
          I assume it's keeping the park
          clean from trash.

                    MAINTENANCE SUPERVISOR
          Yes, and disposing the trash in
          the dumpster behind the restrooms.
          There's extra plastic bags in the
          garage.

                    JOHN
          Is there a lock on the dumpster?

                    MAINTENANCE SUPERVISOR
          Why?

                    JOHN
          Oh, it's not important. I just
          don't want anyone falling inside
          and getting stuck.

                    MAINTENANCE SUPERVISOR
          I've never heard of that happening
          before.

                    JOHN
          Well, that's good.

                    MAINTENANCE SUPERVISOR
          Yes, well, the job pays thirty
          dollars cash per day. Is that
          acceptable?

                    JOHN
          That'll keep me and the dog from
          going hungry.

Both stand up and shake hands across the desk.

                    MAINTENANCE SUPERVISOR
          Welcome aboard! Did I get you
          name?

                    JOHN
          I don't have one yet, but John
          will do for now.

                    MAINTENANCE SUPERVISOR
          As in, John Doe?

                    JOHN
                 (smiling)
          I'd like to think more along the
          line of John Three-Sixteen.

SCENE 29 - EXT. DAY. PARK

There is a series of shots of John picking up trash, tossing
bags into the dumpster, retrieving new bags from the
maintenance garage, etc. There can even be a shot of the dog
helping John by bringing him an empty bottle or can.

While he is working, John observes a couple walking through
the park. The woman is talking/texting on her cell phone.
She then tries to place the cell phone in her back pocket,
but the phone misses her pocket and falls to the ground.
John runs over to retrieve the phone and approaches the
couple, who are now sitting at the same bench where John
once sat. The couple are the same two people who mocked John
and threw their leftover food into the trash can.

> JOHN
> (giving her the phone)
> Excuse me, ma'am, but I saw that
> you dropped your phone.

> PARK WOMAN
> (pleasantly surprised)
> Why thank you, sir!

> JOHN
> No, problem. I'm glad to be of
> service.

> PARK MAN
> Yeah, thanks, dude, she's nuthin
> without her phone.

> JOHN
> Well, I also never got to thank
> you for the food you put in the
> trash can for me.

> PARK WOMAN
> (elbowing the man)
> Billy, apologize to that man for
> what you done!

> PARK MAN
> Oh, dude, was that you? I am so
> sorry for that. Me and my girl
> were having a bad day and I'm
> sorry I took it out on you.

> PARK WOMAN
> Looks like him and me are gonna
> have a bad day today too.

                    JOHN
No need for apologies. I've
forgiven anyone who has slighted
me.

                    PARK MAN
I appreciate that, man. In fact,
I'd like to buy you a proper lunch
today, if you're willin'.

                    JOHN
That won't be necessary, because
I've got a job now. But next time
you see someone down on their
luck, please offer them the meal
that you just offered me.

                    PARK MAN
Will do.

                    JOHN
          (as he walks away)
You two have a nice day.

                    PARK MAN
          (low to woman)
You laughed too when I threw that
food in the trash, so don't act
all high and mighty with me.

                    PARK WOMAN
I laughed at first, but then I
felt bad when I seened the man dig
in the can for our food. I even
prayed God forgive us for
mistreatin' that man... I bet our
meetin' today shows that both the
man and God forgave us.

                    PARK MAN
          (smiling at woman)
Honey, I think you might be right.

After a couple more shots of John working, the scene changes
to show the park fountain. John is sitting on the edge of
the fountain enjoying a drink from a cup, while the dog is
drinking from a makeshift bowl on the ground.

The two teens from the previous fountain scene are seen
creeping up near the fountain.

> FOUNTAIN TEEN TWO
> (to his brother)
> Hey, ain't that the guy we pushed
> in the fountain before?

> FOUNTAIN TEEN ONE
> Sure is... If'n he's so thirsty,
> what say we help him take a big
> gulp from the fountain?

> FOUNTAIN TEEN TWO
> That'd be funny as all out!

The two teens jump out from their hiding place and rush
toward the unsuspecting John. But the dog sees them approach
and starts barking at them. The boys suddenly stop, turn
around, and run away.

> JOHN
> (to the dog)
> Calm down, boy... I wonder what
> those young men wanted...

SCENE 30 - EXT. NIGHT. PARK

John is seen exiting the public restroom with a couple of
garbage bags. He throws the bags in the dumpster.

> JOHN
> (to himself)
> That should do it for the night.

John walks toward the maintenance garage and notices that a
door is open (not the wide garage door for vehicles).

> JOHN (CONT'D)
> (to himself)
> I know I closed that door...

SCENE 31 - INT. NIGHT. MAINTENANCE GARAGE

John approaches the open door and stops in the doorway. He
observes the two fountain teens inside. One is removing a
chainsaw from a shelf.

> FOUNTAIN TEEN TWO
> (to the teen holding the
> chainsaw)
> Okay, let's get out of here!

> JOHN
> (catching them by surprise)
> Hey, what are you guys doing?!

> FOUNTAIN TEEN TWO
> Dammit!

The teen holding the chainsaw suddenly pulls the cord and
starts the saw. The noise from the saw inside the garage is
almost deafening.

> FOUNTAIN TEEN ONE
> (yelling above the noise)
> Git outta our way or I swear I'll
> cut you in half!

John's eyes meet the teen's eyes in a defiant stare. The
teen slowly approaches John with the chainsaw, but John
stands his ground within the doorway.

> FOUNTAIN TEEN ONE (CONT'D)
> I thought I tole you to git out of
> the way!

John's eyes continue to meet the teen's eyes in a defiant
stare. The teen continues to approach John with the
chainsaw, but John continues to stand his ground within the
doorway.

> FOUNTAIN TEEN ONE (CONT'D)
> I ain't kiddin' around! You better
> move yerself before you git cut!

As soon as the blade makes contact with John's shirt, the
chainsaw sputters and stalls.

> FOUNTAIN TEEN ONE (CONT'D)
> (looking down at the stopped
> chainsaw)
> What the...

                    FOUNTAIN TEEN TWO
                (from behind the other teen)
            What happened? Why'd you stop?

                    FOUNTAIN TEEN ONE
            I don't know... maybe the chain
            came off or it ran out of gas...

                    JOHN
            ... Or maybe my Lord and Savior
            Jesus Christ protected me.

                    FOUNTAIN TEEN ONE
            What?

                    JOHN
            You heard me... Now put the saw
            back where you found it.

                    FOUNTAIN TEEN TWO
            Just do it, brother. Put the saw
            back.

                    FOUNTAIN TEEN ONE
            All right, all right, I'll put the
            saw back.

After the teen puts the saw back on the shelf, they both
turn to face John as he the enters the garage.

                    JOHN
                (calmly)
            When I accepted this job, the
            manager said I was responsible for
            everything inside the garage. If
            anything came up missing, I'd
            probably lose my job.

                    FOUNTAIN TEEN ONE
            So you'd rather risk losing your
            life than losing your job?

                    JOHN
            And you'd rather kill someone in
            order to steal an old chainsaw?

                    FOUNTAIN TEEN TWO
          Listen, Mister, we learned our
          lesson, so please let us leave.

                    FOUNTAIN TEEN ONE
          Yeah, we learned our lesson.

                    JOHN
          Let me ask you this first: How
          much money do you think you
          could've got out of that chainsaw?
          Maybe twenty bucks?

                    FOUNTAIN TEEN ONE
          Probably... So what?

                    JOHN
          Because I've got twenty dollars
          right here. If you need it that
          badly, I'd be glad to give it to
          you.

                    FOUNTAIN TEEN TWO
          You'd give us twenty dollars?

                    FOUNTAIN TEEN ONE
          After I just tried to cut you up?

                    JOHN
          If I had more cash, I'd offer you
          more.

                    FOUNTAIN TEEN TWO
                    (tearing up)
          Our mom could sure use the money,
          sir...

John reaches into his pocket and produces a twenty-dollar
bill. He gives it to the closest teen.

                    FOUNTAIN TEEN ONE
                    (accepting the cash)
          Thank you, sir. We have a little
          sister that mom needs to feed.

                    JOHN
          You know, there's plenty of places
          that would hire able-bodied young
          men like you.

> FOUNTAIN TEEN TWO
> That's what our mom keeps sayin',
> but I see now that our way of
> earnin' cash ain't gonna fly no
> more.

> JOHN
> Listen, guys, if you meet me at
> the Mission for the service at
> eight a.m., the Pastor can tell
> you who is hiring around town.

The teen in front turns around to face his brother and nods
to him.

> FOUNTAIN TEEN TWO
> (to John)
> We can do that.

John steps aside and allows the teens to pass.

> JOHN
> (as the teens leave the
> garage)
> I'll see you there...

John kneels down to pray.

> JOHN (CONT'D)
> Dear God, help those boys choose
> the path of righteousness. Amen.

As John stands up, he looks around the garage.

> JOHN (CONT'D)
> (worried look on his face)
> Boy, where are you, boy?!

John begins frantically looking around the interior of the
garage. Finally, he sees the dog crawl out from under a
vehicle or cabinet.

> JOHN (CONT'D)
> (leans down to pet)
> Is this where you've been hiding
> during all the commotion?

SCENE 32 - INT. MORNING. MISSION

John and the Pastor are seated at a table inside the
Mission.

> PASTOR
> So, where have you been staying,
> my son?

> JOHN
> God blessed me with a job as a
> groundskeeper at the City Park.
> The manager allows me to sleep in
> the maintenance garage.

> PASTOR
> Well, you're always welcome here,
> you know that.

> JOHN
> Yes, but if I have a place to
> stay, I don't want to take up a
> bed here if someone needs one.

> PASTOR
> (nods)
> I do appreciate you dropping by
> now and again.

> JOHN
> Yes, and I invited two young men
> to the sermon today. They are
> looking for work and I hope you
> could give them some leads.

> PASTOR
> (laughs)
> Well, as long as they know their
> own names and have social security
> numbers, it'll be a lot easier to
> place them.

> JOHN
> (laughs)
> That's what I figured!

As the two men laugh, the fountain teens approach the table.

> JOHN (CONT'D)
> (looking up at the teens)
> Well, speak of the devil... or
> former devils... Here are the
> young men I was talking about.

                    PASTOR
               (also looking up at the
               teens)
          Gentlemen, please take a seat!

The teens shyly sit down.

                    FOUNTAIN TEEN TWO
          I hope we ain't delayin' your
          service any.

                    PASTOR
          The sermon can wait. The Lord has
          more pressing work for me to do.

                    JOHN
          Yes, I'm glad you could make it,
          guys.

                    FOUNTAIN TEEN ONE
          Mom was grateful for the money you
          gave us.

                    JOHN
          No problem.

                    PASTOR
          So, are you boys still in school?

                    FOUNTAIN TEEN TWO
          Not right now, because of summer
          break. But this fall, I'll be a
          Junior and my brother here will be
          a Senior.

                    PASTOR
          That's great! So, as far as
          working hours, I guess you'd be
          pretty flexible until school
          starts.

                    FOUNTAIN TEEN ONE
               (softly, while looking down)
          I don't think it'll matter...

                    PASTOR
          Why do you say that?

                    FOUNTAIN TEEN TWO
          Because we don't think anyone
          would want people like us working
          for them.

FOUNTAIN TEEN ONE
Yes, nobody wants us. Not even our
father wants anything to do with
us.

FOUNTAIN TEEN TWO
(sadly)

Before he left us, our dad said we
was all worthless and didn't want
to see us no more.

JOHN
I can assure you, you're not
worthless to God.

PASTOR
Your friend here is right. You're
not worthless. Not to God, and not
to either of us. We see your
potential and that's why we want
to help you.

FOUNTAIN TEEN ONE
(tearing up)
Well, we ain't no good in school
neither. We barely pass each
grade. So, who would want to hire
a couple of dummies?

PASTOR
(looks at fountain teen two)
My son, do you think your brother
is dumb?

FOUNTAIN TEEN TWO
'Course not!

JOHN
(looks at fountain teen one)
And do you think he's a dummy?

FOUNTAIN TEEN ONE
No, but other people think we are,
because we don't do good in
school. Even the teachers say
they're just pushin' us through to
git rid of us.

PASTOR
Don't concern yourself with what
other people think.

                    JOHN
          Yes, instead of dwelling over what
          other people think, you should be
          spending your time proving them
          wrong. Your priority right now
          should be helping your mother. It
          sounds like she needs you guys
          even more than you might believe.

                  FOUNTAIN TEEN TWO
                  (through tears)
          That's why we decided to come here
          after you helped us out.

Fountain Teen One suddenly grabs John's hand on the table
and rests his forehead on it.

                  FOUNTAIN TEEN ONE
                  (desperately)
          Please forgive me for wanting to
          hurt you! I am so sorry! I wish I
          was dead!

                    JOHN
                  (crying as he places his
                  other hand on the back of
                  the teen's head)
          My God, boy, don't ever say that!
          All is forgiven from last night.

                    PASTOR
                  (grabbing the hand of teen
                  two)
          Yes, my sons, you are both good in
          the eyes of the Lord!

                  FOUNTAIN TEEN TWO
          Can we be excused for a moment?

                    PASTOR
          Of course... You're welcome to
          wait for us in the chapel.

The sobbing teens leave the table and head for the chapel.

                  PASTOR (CONT'D)
                  (to John after the teens
                  have left)
          I don't know what happened last
          night - and maybe I don't want to
          know.

                    JOHN
          Believe me, you don't...

SCENE 33 - INT. DAY. MISSION CHAPEL

John and the teens are seated in the front row of the chapel. The camera focuses on the Pastor at the pulpit/podium.

> PASTOR
> (looking down occasionally
> at his notes)

Even though He had done many good deeds and had helped many people, Jesus was not initially regarded as the Son of God.

His fellow Jews ignored His righteous acts and tried to use His words against Him.

While attending a celebration inside a temple, other Jews demanded that He declare Himself the Son of God. Jesus answered, "The works that I do in my Father's name bear witness about me, but you do not believe because you are not among my sheep. My sheep hear my voice, and I know them, and they follow me. I give them eternal life, and they will never perish, and no one will snatch them out of my hand. My Father, who has given them to me, is greater than all, and no one is able to snatch them out of the Father's hand. I and the Father are one."

When Jesus left the temple, His detractors followed Him outside. They had taken issue with Jesus's comment that He and the Father are One. They began to collect rocks with the intention to stone Jesus to death.

Jesus faced the angry men with the stones and said, "I have shown you many good works from the Father; for which of them are you going to stone me?" The men answered, "It is not for good work that we are going to stone you; but for blasphemy, because you, being a man, call yourself God."

Jesus responded by asking, "Do you
say of him whom the Father
consecrated and sent into the
world, 'You are blaspheming,'
because I said, 'I am the Son of
God'? If I am not doing the works
of my Father, then do not believe
me; but if I do them, even though
you do not believe me, believe the
works, that you may know and
understand that the Father is in
me and I am in the Father."

The angry men then looked at one
another and realized that no one
wanted to cast the first stone, so
they dropped their rocks and
allowed Jesus to leave unmolested.

                    PASTOR (CONT'D)
             (opening a bible)
That story is from John, Chapter
Ten. Jesus had more to say in this
Chapter, which I would like to
read to you now:

"Truly, truly, I say to you, he
who does not enter the sheepfold
by the door but climbs in by
another way, that man is a thief
and a robber. But he who enters by
the door is the shepherd of the
sheep. To him the gatekeeper
opens. The sheep hear his voice,
and he calls his own sheep by name
and leads them out. When he has
brought out all his own, he goes
before them, and the sheep follow
him, for they know his voice. A
stranger they will not follow, but
they will flee from him, for they
do not know the voice of
strangers."

PASTOR (CONT'D)

"I am the door of the sheep. All
who came before me are thieves and
robbers, but the sheep did not
listen to them. I am the door. If
anyone enters by me, he will be
saved and will go in and out and
find pasture. The thief comes only
to steal and kill and destroy. I
came that they may have life and
have it abundantly. I am the good
shepherd. The good shepherd lays
down his life for the sheep. He
who is a hired hand and not a
shepherd, who does not own the
sheep, sees the wolf coming and
leaves the sheep and flees, and
the wolf snatches them and
scatters them. He flees because he
is a hired hand and cares nothing
for the sheep. I am the good
shepherd. I know my own and my own
know me, just as the Father knows
me and I know the Father; and I
lay down my life for the sheep.
And I have other sheep that are
not of this fold. I must bring
them also, and they will listen to
my voice. So there will be one
flock, one shepherd. For this
reason, the Father loves me,
because I lay down my life that I
may take it up again. No one takes
it from me, but I lay it down of
my own accord. I have authority to
lay it down, and I have authority
to take it up again. This charge I
have received from my Father."

PASTOR (CONT'D)
(closing the bible)
Amen.

The Pastor descends from the pulpit/podium and meets with
the teens and John in the front row.

SCENE 34 - EXT. DAY. PARK

Shots of John and the dog working in the park. John looks up
when he hears a woman scream. The woman happens to be the
same woman who John approached at the bus stop.

                    MISCELLANEOUS WOMAN
                      (screaming)
               Help! That man just took my purse!

John sees the man running away with the woman's purse, drops
his trash picker and bag, and gives pursuit. The dog is also
giving chase and is initially running in front of John. But
a wide shot shows John running furiously past the dog.

When John is close enough to the thief, he tackles the man
from behind. The dog catches up and begins barking as the
men struggle on the ground.

John soon manages to turn the thief over on the ground and
gets on top of the thief. John looks down at the thief's
face.

                         THIEF
                       (desperate)
               Okay, okay, I give up! I don't
               want the purse! Please don't hurt
               me!

John is staring down at the man's face and does not respond.

                    THIEF (CONT'D)
               Let me go! What's wrong with you
               anyway?

John continues to stare down at the man's face without
responding.

                    THIEF (CONT'D)
               Are you some kinda psycho or
               something? Let me up!

                         JOHN
               I know you.

                         THIEF
               What?

                         JOHN
               I know you from somewhere.

                         THIEF
               You don't know me! Just take the
               stupid purse and leave me alone!

SCENE 35 - EXT. NIGHT. STREET

In a black and white flashback, John is changing a tire on
his car under a streetlight. Some thugs approach John from
the shadows and one kicks him to the ground. The thief in
the park then picks up the fallen tire iron and swings it at
John's head. John clearly sees the thief's face before all
fades to black.

SCENE 36 - EXT. DAY. PARK

After the flashback, John is still on top of the thief.

>   JOHN
>   But I do know you.

>   THIEF
>   From where? How do you know me?

>   JOHN
>   (staring into the thief's
>   eyes)
>   One night I was changing my tire
>   and you hit me with a tire iron.

The thief turns pale and becomes frightened, shaking under
John weight.

>   THIEF
>   (stuttering)
>   D-d-dude... Oh my god, I-I am so
>   sorry. I didn't mean to hit you
>   that hard, I swear.

>   JOHN
>   (angry)
>   I lost my memory because... No, I
>   lost my life because of you. I
>   ended up under a bridge and I
>   didn't know who I was... I still
>   don't know.

>   THIEF
>   (desperate)
>   Listen, I know I did wrong and I
>   am truly sorry. But let me try to
>   make it up to you. Please don't
>   kill me.

>   JOHN
>   (lightening up)
>   I'm not going to kill you.

>   THIEF
>   Oh, god, thank you...

>   JOHN
>   I do need your help.

>   THIEF
>   Anything... Anything I can do...

>   JOHN
>   Do you have my wallet or my
>   identification?

>   THIEF
>   No, man. We threw that all away,
>   including the credit cards. We
>   just took the cash... I'm sorry.

>   JOHN
>   Okay. So at least tell me what
>   street I was on.

>   THIEF
>   I think it was on Fifth Street,
>   near the market... Yeah, I'm
>   pretty sure it was Fifth Street.

>   JOHN
>   Good... Can you tell me what kind
>   of car I was driving?

>   THIEF
>   That I'm not so sure about... It
>   was dark. But the car was some
>   kind of light-colored sedan...
>   Maybe a Toyota, but I can't say
>   for sure.

John pulls his arm back like he is going to punch the
thief in the head, but at the last second, he pulls back.

>   JOHN
>   (gritting his teeth)
>   You know, it's ironic, but if you
>   hadn't hurt me, I would not now
>   have the capacity to forgive you.

>   THIEF
>   (befuddled)
>   W-what?

John rolls off the man, grabs the purse and stands up. As
John and the dog walk away, the camera catches the thief
crawling off in the distance.

John finds the distraught woman sitting on a bench. He hands
her the purse.

>   JOHN
>   Here's your purse, ma'am.

                    MISCELLANEOUS WOMAN
                 (looks up at John with tears
                  in her eyes)

Oh, thank you, kind sir! I wish
there were more men like you! How
can I re-pay you? Do you need any
cash?

                    JOHN
                 (as he walks away)
The time to help me was at the bus
stop.

                    MISCELLANEOUS WOMAN
                 (confused)
The bus stop?

SCENE 37 - EXT. DAY. CITY SIDEWALK

A few shots of John and the dog walking on various
sidewalks. They eventually come to the Fifth Street market.

                    JOHN
                (down to the dog)
            Well, boy, it looks like my car
            has been towed.

John walks into the market while the dog waits outside.

SCENE 38 - INT. DAY. MARKET

John walks into the market and approaches the counter.

          JOHN
        (to the clerk)
Excuse me... My car broke down
outside your market a few days
ago. Can you tell me what may have
happened to it?

        MARKET CLERK
Can you tell me why you abandoned
it?

          JOHN
Well, I didn't really abandon it.
I was attacked by thugs while I
was changing a tire.

        MARKET CLERK
I guess that explains all the
blood.

          JOHN
      (cringes and touches the top
      of his head)

Obviously, I managed to walk
away, but I don't remember much
else about that night.

        MARKET CLERK
I want you to know that I did wait
a while for the owner to return
before I called the towing
company.

          JOHN
I appreciate that.

        MARKET CLERK
And you was in a No Parking zone.

          JOHN
I didn't realize... But I'm not
questioning your decision to call
a tow truck.

        MARKET CLERK
Then why are you here? I doubt
it's for the fresh produce.

                    JOHN
          Maybe you could tell me what tow
          company you called.

                    MARKET CLERK
          The apples are fresh off the truck
          this morning.

                    JOHN
          I'm sure they are, but I need to
          find my car. Certainly, you
          remember what towing company you
          called.

                    MARKET CLERK
          Towing company?

                    JOHN
          Yes, sir, which one?

                    MARKET CLERK
          Well, the same one I always call!

                    JOHN
          And that is?

                    MARKET CLERK
          'Cause of that No Parking zone,
          I'm calling for tows all the time.

                    JOHN
          Sir, is there a reason you won't
          tell me the name of the company.

                    MARKET CLERK
          'Course not! It's Monroe Towing.
          It's the closest one to my store,
          so I use them mostly.

                    JOHN
          Exactly how close to the store, if
          you don't mind me asking?

                    MARKET CLERK
          Just a couple blocks up Fifth,
          then turn left on Monroe Avenue.

                    JOHN
          Thank you.

                    MARKET CLERK
          I figger it's called Monroe Towing
          because they're located on Monroe
          Avenue.

                    JOHN
          You've been very helpful...

                    MARKET CLERK
          Sure you don't want to grab any
          fresh apples or oranges for your
          trip?

                    JOHN
          No thank you, I'm a little short
          on funds right now... but maybe
          you could help me with the color
          or model.

                    MARKET CLERK
          Of the apples?

                    JOHN
          No, of the car that was towed.

                    MARKET CLERK
          You don't know the color or model
          of yer own car?

                    JOHN
          Friend, after I was struck on the
          head with a tire iron, I don't
          even remember my own name.

                    MARKET CLERK
          Oh, sorry, I didn't think it was
          that bad... Your car was a white
          Toyota Camry.

                    JOHN
          Thanks so much! I hope the tow
          company still has it on the lot!

                    MARKET CLERK
          No problem. Please grab a fresh
          apple on your way out. It's on the
          house.

SCENE 39 - EXT. DAY. CITY SIDEWALK

Shot of John walking along, chomping on an apple. Pan down
to show the dog carrying an apple in its mouth.

> JOHN
> It shouldn't be too much farther,
> boy... I see Monroe Avenue just
> ahead.

John and the dog turn left at the corner and walk until they
approach a huge junk yard.

> JOHN (CONT'D)
> I think this might be the place!

John enters the tow company lobby. The dog waits outside,
attempting to eat its apple.

SCENE 40 - INT. DAY. TOW COMPANY

John approaches the counter.

> TOW CLERK
> (glancing up momentarily
> from a computer screen)
> What d'ya need?

> JOHN
> Ah, yes, I was hoping you could
> help me.

> TOW CLERK
> (not looking up from the
> screen)
> How's that?

> JOHN
> A few days ago, the market on
> Fifth Street called you to tow
> away a white Camry.

> TOW CLERK
> (not looking up from the
> screen)
> So?

> JOHN
> So, the car belongs to me.

> TOW CLERK
> (not looking up from the
> screen)
> You come to pay the tow fee?

> JOHN
> (pauses)
> Well, not necessarily...

> TOW CLERK
> (finally looking John in the
> eyes)
> Then I can't help you.

> JOHN
> But you don't understand...

The tow clerk returns to looking at the computer, typing a few things in the process.

> JOHN (CONT'D)
> Excuse me...

A phone rings on the counter and the clerk picks up the receiver.

>   TOW CLERK
>   (into the phone)
>   Monroe Towing, how may I help
>   you?... Yes, we're located on
>   Monroe Avenue... Sorry to hear
>   that... I hope there were no
>   injuries... Yes, we know where
>   that is... We can certainly get
>   over there, but all our trucks are
>   busy at present... It might be an
>   hour before we can reach you, is
>   that okay?... Yes, we'll do our
>   best to get there as soon as
>   possible, ma'am... Bye.

The clerk hangs up the phone and reaches into his pocket for
his cell phone.

>   JOHN
>   As I was saying...

The clerk puts the cell phone up to his ear.

>   TOW CLERK
>   Yeah, Jack. A lady just called in
>   from an accident on Eighth and
>   Jefferson. What would be your ETA,
>   if you don't already have a
>   vehicle in tow?... Yeah, you can
>   finish your meal. There's no
>   rush... I told her about an hour,
>   but she'll just have to wait until
>   you get there... Beggars can't be
>   choosers... Ha!... Thanks... Bye.

John is shown with a shocked look on his face as the clerk
puts the cell phone back in his pocket. The clerk
immediately begins typing on the computer again.

John clears his throat.

The clerk looks up from the computer.

>   TOW CLERK (CONT'D)
>   You still here?

>   JOHN
>   Well, yeah, I mean you have my car
>   somewhere on your lot...

>   TOW CLERK
>   Like I said, buddy, no fee, no
>   car, no exceptions... Now if
>   you'll excuse me, I have work to
>   do.

                    JOHN
         Can I at least tell you what's
         going on with the car?

                  TOW CLERK
              (rolls his eyes)
         Okay, but make it quick, 'cause I
         don't got all day.

                    JOHN
         All right, a few nights ago I got
         a flat tire on Fifth Street and
         when I started to fix the flat, I
         got jumped by some hoodlums. They
         cracked my skull with a tire iron
         and took everything I had. Somehow
         I ended up underneath a bridge
         with a bunch of homeless people.
         One of them tried to steal my
         boots. Anyway, I soon realized
         that I had amnesia and couldn't
         remember who I was or even where I
         was. I tried asking some folks,
         but a cop picked me up for
         panhandling and I was tossed in a
         cell with a bunch of inmates who
         thought I was a gang-banger. The
         next day, the judge threw me out
         of the courtroom because he
         thought I was trying to scam the
         government. Then I got pushed in a
         fountain...

                  TOW CLERK
              (interrupting)
         I thought I told you to keep it
         short, buddy.

                    JOHN
         I'm trying. I just want you to
         know what I've been going
         through...

                  TOW CLERK
         Is this some kind of a joke? Are
         you secretly filming me for a
         viral video prank or something?

                    JOHN
         What? No. I'm being serious and
         I'm hoping you can show me a
         little empathy for my dire
         situation.

                  TOW CLERK
         Okay, bud, what is it you want me

to do?

                    JOHN
Can you at least look up the VIN
on the white Toyota Camry that was
recently towed?

               TOW CLERK
               (smiling)
No, I cannot.

                    JOHN
Excuse me?

               TOW CLERK
               (smirking)
You heard me... Now be on your way
and have a nice day.

                    JOHN
What?... Why?... Why can't you do
that for me?

               TOW CLERK
Because I don't know you from
Adam... You don't have any ID but
you want me to search the DMV
database to find the owner of a
car.

                    JOHN
Yes, considering my current
plight, that is exactly what I'd
like you to do.

               TOW CLERK
Well, you can fergit it! How do I
know you don't work for the
government and you're testing me
to see if I'd hand out
confidential registration
information?

                    JOHN
Seriously?

               TOW CLERK
Yes, seriously. Now git your sorry
self outta my place of business
before I call the cops.

                    JOHN
               (starting to walk away)
Go ahead and call the cops. I'll
be waiting outside. Maybe they'll
help me.

                    TOW CLERK
                (calling after John as he is
                 leaving)
            Yeah, and maybe the cops'll throw
            you back in the slammer where you
            belong.

After John leaves, the clerk walks up to the door and locks
it from inside. He also flips over a sign on the door to
indicate that the office is CLOSED.

                    TOW CLERK (CONT'D)
                (to himself)
            I ain't calling no cops. I don't
            need them snooping around here.

SCENE 41 - EXT. DAY. CITY SIDEWALK

John meets up again with the dog on the sidewalk. He looks
down at the dog.

>   JOHN
>   You eat that whole apple, core and
>   all?

The dog barks in response.

>   JOHN (CONT'D)
>   (to the dog)
>   Come on, boy, let's walk around
>   the perimeter to see if I can
>   locate my car... If the cops come,
>   then I can tell them exactly where
>   it is. Hopefully, they'll believe
>   me and try to help.

John and the dog begin walking around the chain-link
fenced-in perimeter, stopping every once in a while for John
to peer into the yard at the multiple vehicles within.

At one point, John gazes through the fence for a longer
period of time. He becomes excited.

>   JOHN (CONT'D)
>   Hey, boy, I think I see it! I
>   mean, I think I recognize it! My
>   car! It's right over there, behind
>   that motorcycle!

The dog picks up on John's excitement and begins to bark.

>   JOHN (CONT'D)
>   I wish I could just get in
>   there... I wish I could just sit
>   in that car for a few minutes...
>   Maybe it would all come back to
>   me!

As soon as John puts his hands up to grasp the fence, like
he is going to climb it, a vicious junkyard-type dog runs up
on the other side and begins growling and gnashing its teeth
toward John. John's dog begins barking at the junkyard dog.
John let's go of his grip on the fence and backs away.

>   JOHN (CONT'D)
>   (to his dog)
>   Let's get out of here, boy, before
>   the guy inside hears all the
>   barking.

John and the dog run across the street and disappear in a residential neighborhood.

                    JOHN (CONT'D)
                (slowing down to a walk)
            We can always go back later...
            Maybe someone else will be
            working.

SCENE 42 - EXT. DUSK. RESIDENTIAL SIDEWALK

Now there are shots of John and the dog as they walk
casually through various residential neighborhoods. People
are mowing lawns, washing cars and performing other normal
activities around their homes. Some kids are riding bikes on
the street and playing in yards.

                    JOHN
                (to the dog)
            Remember we need to get back to
            the park by nightfall.

John and the dog walk past an electric pole that has a
tattered paper sign attached to it. They continue walking.
Suddenly, John stops.

                    JOHN (CONT'D)
            Hold on, boy. I want to check
            something.

John walks back to the pole and opens up the tattered paper
sign.

                    JOHN (CONT'D)
            Oh, no...

The camera catches the contents of the Lost Dog sign, which
has a picture of a dog that looks like John's dog.

The dog walks up to John and looks up at him as he studies
the sign.

                    JOHN (CONT'D)
                (glancing down at the dog)
            It looks a little bit like you,
            boy, but I can't be sure... The
            picture is all faded from the
            sun... It says 111 Elm Street...
            Maybe we should see if someone's
            been looking for you.

John and the dog walk to the corner and notice the street
sign for Elm Street. They walk down Elm Street, looking at
the numbers on the houses.

Suddenly they are standing in front of a house with the
number 111.

                    JOHN (CONT'D)
                  (looks down at the dog)
              I kind of hope it's not you, but
              let's go check.

John and the dog approach the front door of the house. John
lightly knocks upon the door.

In a few moments, the door slowly opens to reveal a young
girl, probably aged ten or eleven.

The camera shows the girl's face light up. She turns her
head to yell at someone inside the house.

                    GIRL
                  (yelling)
              Momma, momma... Daddy brought our
              dog home!

John's face is crushed with emotion and he falls to his
knees. He throws his arms in the air and looks up to the
heavens.

                    JOHN
                  (screams)
              Oh, my God, thank you for bringing
              me home!!!

The camera is now above the home (drone shot?), looking down
upon John as the girl runs out to hug her wailing father.
The dog is joyfully jumping on both of them.

Fade to black.

The end.

Rich Bottles Jr.

08-29-2020

ABOUT THE AUTHOR

After an unillustrious print journalism career in southwestern Pennsylvania, Rich Bottles Jr. moved to West Virginia at the age of 32 to pursue a career in technical writing.

He spends his free time visiting and hiking at the many state parks in the Mountain State, which is also where he develops the concepts for his novels. He has produced a trilogy of WV-themed "humorrorotica" books, the most recent of which is *The Manacled*, set in the vicinity of the West Virginia Penitentiary. Other books in the series include *Lumberjacked* and *Hellhole West Virginia*.

STRANGE
FRIENDS

GARY LEE VINCENT

PROVE YOUR LOVE

GARY LEE VINCENT